CRAFTING DECEPTION

Gasper's Cove Mysteries Book 2

BARBARA EMODI

C&T PUBLISHING
Another Maker Inspired!

Text copyright © 2023 by Barbara Emodi

Artwork copyright © 2023 by C&T Publishing, Inc.

Publisher: Amy Barrett-Daffin

Creative Director: Gailen Runge

Senior Editor: Roxane Cerda

Cover Designer: Mariah Sinclair

Book Designer: April Mostek

Production Coordinator: Zinnia Heinzmann

Illustrator: Emilija Mihajlov

Published by C&T Publishing, Inc., P.O. Box 1456, Lafayette, CA 94549

Library of Congress Control Number: 2023945622

Printed in the USA

10 9 8 7 6 5 4 3 2 1

Gasper's Cove Mysteries Series

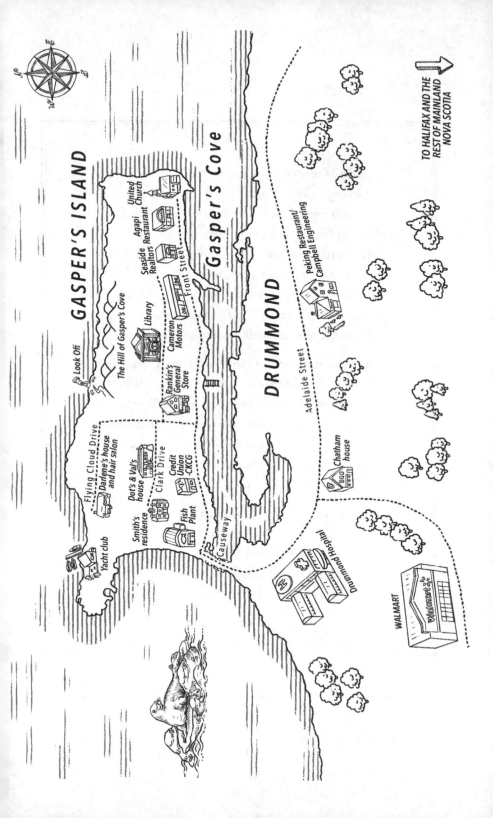

Rankin's General store has served the community of Gasper's Cove, Nova Scotia, since 1920. To this day, it is owned and operated by members of the Rankin family. For many years, the store was the only retail operation in the community, supplying boat supplies, tools, and grocery staples. More recently, the second floor of the store has also housed the Gasper's Cove Crafters: A Community Co-op, selling locally made arts and crafts.

The building has remained as it was originally built, with only structural maintenance. Visitors can now enjoy the exquisite, pressed-metal ceiling and the expert craftsmanship that went into building the counters, display cabinets, and shelving throughout the store, which have been maintained in their original state.

As an example of both commercial and community life representative of the vigor of Nova Scotia's coastal communities, the store has been designated a protected historical property by the Province of Nova Scotia.

**PLAQUE PROPERTY OF
THE NOVA SCOTIA HERITAGE SOCIETY**

Reviews

★ ★ ★ ★ ★ *After seeing this place on the Tourism Nova Scotia website, we took a spin over on a recent trip up the coast. Worth it. Many unique craft items upstairs, could hardly get my wife out of there.*

★ ★ ★ ★ ★ *This place is nuts. Stopped to see if they carried wax for my surfboard (they did) but also lots of stuff I swear has been on the shelves for a hundred years. Dude behind the counter knows a lot about Carl Jung. Stopping on our way back.*

★ ★ ★ ★ ★ *Makes me want to move to Nova Scotia. A lady in the co-op showed me a new way to do heels on socks and they have a small sewing school on the main floor! Decided to stay over the weekend for a bag-making workshop.*

★ *Don't know where the health inspector is, definitely avoid if you are allergic to animals. This place has a ratty old chair inside the front door with a big dog on it. Saw a cat asleep on a stack of towels. No Wi-Fi. Staff too chatty. If you are in a hurry, take my advice and go to the Walmart in Drummond across the causeway.*

PROLOGUE

HMS EMERALD, SEPTEMBER 1939

Ordinary Seamen Jones and Mowat stared down.

"This is the top-secret mission? Bars of soap?"

"Don't be daft, mate. Don't you know gold when you see it?"

"Gold? That's the cargo going across the Atlantic to Canada. What for?"

"Where have you been? There's a war on. Her Majesty's government needs to buy arms from the Yanks."

"Well, my lad, what's the big plan? It was your idea to drop the crate to see what was in it. What do we do now? We can't nick it."

"True enough. They'll count the bars for sure. But hang on, what's this? There's a pouch underneath, at the side. Almost missed it."

"Come on, what do you see? What's in it?"

"Not sure. Looks like some old rubbish jewelry to me, but if it wasn't valuable, it wouldn't be here. Get a move on, help me nail these boards back."

"You're keeping it?"

"Safekeeping's more like it. I know just the spot we can stow it until we dock in Halifax. Some blokes there will buy anything. Might as well have something for our troubles," Mowat said.

Jones smiled and picked up a hammer.

No one would ever know.

CHAPTER ONE

"How about this? Voodoo knife, gently used?" Annette's flowered pen was poised above a card.

"You are a genius," I said. "Do it. How else are we going to get rid of an old carving knife?" That settled, I reached into the bin of textiles, my specialty, and pulled out a cotton rectangle. "Now who would donate a tea towel with rust stains on it?" I asked the room.

Annette put down her pen and moved in for a closer look; as manager, she was in charge of quality control. "Hydrogen peroxide, that's what you need. Those are old blood stains, but that will take them out. Trust me, I have boys."

"How about we sell them together? The knife and the bloody tea towel. Make them a set?" Catherine suggested. For the town librarian, she was an unexpectedly inventive volunteer. It was her idea to attach quirky note cards to our hard-to-identify items before we put them out on the shelves of the Recreate and Recycle Depot.

"Sure. Can you do that, Darlene?" I asked my cousin and best friend. There was no response.

I waved my hand in front of Darlene's unfocused eyes. "You okay?" I asked. Our shift was almost done, and then I was back to the Crafter's Co-op. We had to keep moving.

Darlene shook her henna waves and met my eyes. "Sorry, I have a lot on my mind."

"Like what?"

Darlene reached for a folding chair behind our communal worktable and sat down. "My mother is trying to kill me," she said.

"What? Why would you even say that?" This made no sense. All the time I was growing up, I thought my aunt Colleen was the perfect mother. I'd wanted to live in her house instead of in the spotless order of mine, her home had a different project in every room—a glue gun plugged in on the kitchen counter, a pattern pinned to fabric on the ping-pong table in the basement, unconnected granny squares on the backseat of the car, and half-done mittens on the arm of the recliner. Colleen seemed incapable of *not* making things, but as I got older, it became clear to me that women like her did crafts precisely so they *didn't* kill anyone. In her case, that would have been my uncle, a charming man who did "this and that," and her seven reckless just-like-their-father boys. I was sure Colleen wasn't out to murder her daughter, the only responsible member of the family besides herself.

Darlene stared up at the metal trusses in the ceiling of the building, here on the edge of Drummond's industrial park, and sighed.

"It's the move," she said. "I'm down to my last nerve. Now that Dad's gone, Mom can't keep living alone at the end of that road. Coming into town is for her own good. But I swear, by the time we get that house cleared out, there will be nothing left of me."

My phone buzzed in my pocket. I ignored it. This was more important.

It buzzed again.

"Can you be specific?" Catherine asked. "What's the problem?"

Darlene swept her eyes around the jumbled mess of the Depot's intake room as she struggled to explain. "The house is like this place, but worse. She saved everything."

I picked up some lace yardage and pulled it straight along the measuring tape on the side of the table. Darlene's mother taught me to sew when I was eight. I still used those skills in the sewing classes I taught. What could I say in her defense?

"Maybe your mom doesn't want to see her whole life lined up in garbage bags along the road," I suggested. "She was raised when it was a sin to waste anything. Tell her to donate. Look around here."

Annette agreed with me. "Listen, that's what we did with Mom's jewelry collection. She sold Avon for forty years and owned every piece of jewelry they ever put out. We gave up trying to figure out what to do with it, so we took our pick and brought the rest in here. It just made sense."

Darlene stared at the bins around us, filled to the top with remnants of fabric, beads, craft loom bands, faded embroidery transfers, tufts of wool roving, and abandoned quilt pieces.

"You don't get it. Mom wants to dole it out. She's obsessed. Do I want the plate the Girl Guides gave her when she was commissioner in 1967? Do I want the flannelette for the pajamas she cut out when I was six?" Darlene's eyes went glassy with tears. Catherine pulled a neatly folded tissue out of the pocket of her jeans, the denim faded along the pressing marks down the legs, and handed it to her.

Darlene sniffed. "If I say no, I don't want it, she says someone might, it's still good, hangs up, and phones the boys. Then, my brothers call me to say make her stop bugging us. I can't take much more of this."

Catherine snorted in a very un-librarian-like way. "It's always the daughter who gets stuck with the work," she said, with the authority of someone who had been there herself. "Nothing causes trouble in a family like possessions. Two of my aunts are still not speaking because one of them sold my grandmother's Singer Featherweight." We considered this. Maybe the angry aunt had a point; those machines had a beautiful straight stitch.

"It's so hard being the only girl," Darlene continued, her hands twisting purple rickrack into a looped figure eight between her French manicured fingers. "The boys are useless. They only did the garage in case Granddad hid booze in there during his rum-running days, but that's it." Her voice rose with desperation. "Mom keeps saying, 'I'll make a pile.' Do you know how many piles there are in that house? If we ever had to call the paramedics, all they'd find would be a little old lady buried under a thousand tiny balls of leftover yarn."

"There's your answer right there," Catherine said. "You've just got to get through to her that what she gives away might be useful to someone."

Catherine was right. "Good point," I said. Why, just past the doors of this room, customers were waiting to buy donated sewing machines, checked by someone named Ralph, "working moderate, foot pedal not too bad," bundles of old *National Geographics*, a fur stole with one mink eye missing, and matted wigs. No one should ever underestimate the creative consumer's ability to see potential in just about anything.

Darlene was unconvinced. "I'll talk to her, not that it will do much good."

I started to argue but was interrupted when Annette tossed a loose cloud of fabric onto the middle of the worktable.

"Val, you're the sewing teacher. What's this? Silk?" Annette asked, spreading out a large thin sheet of yellowed fabric, tightly woven, with flat-felled seams along its length.

"Hang on," I said, moving quickly across the room, a prospector spotting a gold nugget in a stream of polyester remnants. I reached out and rubbed an edge between my thumb and fingers. "I think you're right. It's silk."

"It's made into something. What is it?" Darlene asked. "A sail?"

Catherine raised her glasses from the chain around her neck and lifted a corner of the fabric to have a closer look. "No, it's not a sail. Do you know what this is? It's an old parachute from the war. The harness has been cut off, but look, it still has a few of the D rings."

I stared at her. "Are you serious? A parachute? How do you know?"

"I've seen these in books," Catherine said, letting her glasses fall onto her Liberty print blouse. "I'm sure that's what it is, from World War II. The men brought the parachutes home, and the girls made wedding dresses from them. My mother's sister was married in one. She used the same parachute that saved her fiancé's life when he was shot down. They had to sew appliqués over the bullet holes."

This was our heritage, resourceful women. "Just think, it was the only fabric they had to work with," I said. "Kind of sad and happy at the same time. But how did something like that end up here, in a small town on the coast of Nova Scotia?"

Catherine shrugged. "Who knows? Bit of a mystery. But the point is, we can't put this out to sell. It's an artifact. I'll take it," she said, reaching for the fabric. "I'll find out where we should send it. They'd know at the Archives in Halifax."

"Hang on," Darlene said, no longer interested in her mother's move. "Do you think we're looking at a tragic love story?" she whispered, laying a reverent hand on the fabric. "Maybe some bride saved this silk for a wedding dress she never made." She bent down. "Look, there are numbers and a word stenciled on the hem at the bottom. It's blurry, but I can still read it. 'Fairy' something. How sweet is that?"

"Very sweet," I said, cutting Darlene off. My cousin's three marriages had not ended well, but she remained a romantic, something I'd left behind a long time ago. I was more intrigued by the parachute's strange arrival in this room. "If only objects could talk," I said. "I wonder who dropped this off."

"I can ask," offered Annette. "We take donations every Tuesday. Next time she's in, I'll ask the lady who handles it if she knows anything."

"Would you?" I said. "There's a story there, and I'd love to know what it is." My phone buzzed in my pocket again. Who was trying so hard to reach me?

I pulled out my phone and looked down. There were six texts from Rollie, another cousin, and manager of Rankin's General, our family store over in Gasper's Cove.

Bad news. Found Waldo.

Waldo. That would be Wally Butt from "Wally's Authentic Celtic Tours," a man as famous for fabricating the facts he told tourists as for getting lost. The locals had nicknamed him "Where's Waldo" Butt. But where had Rollie found Waldo?

Good news. He brought friends.

Rollie meant customers. One of Wally's tours had landed at the store.

Bad news. They're running around in the Co-op.

Rats. Rollie had no idea how to work the vintage cash register on the second floor.

Need more hands on deck. Polly at school.

Not good. Thirteen-year-old Polly, the store's unofficial helper, wouldn't be there until the bus dropped her off at 3:30, and Donald "Duck" MacDonald, our ex-con handyman, was probably waiting out the tour's visit down in the basement with Shadow, the store cat.

There was no need to listen to the voicemail. Rollie, a lovely man but no retailer, was alone with a liar on wheels and tourists rifling through our crafts.

I tapped back as quickly as I could.

> Hang on.
>
> Don't let anything happen.
>
> On our way.

I looked at all the donations still to be sorted, and then at Darlene. "Crisis across the causeway," I whispered.

Darlene did a mental translation—she knew this meant time for a Rollie rescue. "Let's hustle," she said, grabbing her purse from behind a stack of jackets and following me out the door to the parking lot out front.

Once we were settled in the car and Darlene had snapped on her seatbelt, she looked over at me. "There's a name for it, on the tip of my tongue," she said.

Distracted, I flipped on my left turn signal, ready to turn onto the road that led over the water to Gasper's Cove. Fifteen minutes tops and we'd be there. How much could happen in fifteen minutes?

"Name for what?"

"Like my aunt's chair," Darlene said.

Where did that come from? "Chair? Darlene, you have a lot of aunts, and they have a lot of chairs."

"Frank's wife, that aunt, you know, the fancy one in her entry? They found it on the beach, set up on the rocks like someone had been sitting there and got up and walked away," Darlene persisted. "You know what I mean, don't you? A thing that washes ashore, and they never know where it came from? What do they call it?"

"Not a clue," I said, which was true.

Darlene held her bag tightly on her lap and stared out the window down at the water on either side of the short land bridge we called the causeway that connected the town of Drummond to our little community.

Her head snapped up. "Got it. I remember," she said, pleased with herself.

I looked over.

"What is it?" I asked.

"Ghost gear," Darlene said. "They call it ghost gear."

CHAPTER TWO

As Darlene and I left Drummond behind and headed into Gasper's Cove, I felt the familiar lift of going home. I had no idea what Darlene was talking about with chairs and ghosts on beaches, but then again Nova Scotia was a tricky province. Our weather taught us that. Sometimes, during the long, gray, icy winters, I wondered why anyone lived here. Then, spring would come, the air felt like champagne, the ocean shimmered, and I would decide there was no more beautiful place on Earth. But somewhere in the background, I would hear Nature muttering under her breath, "Got you again." This was no place for those who weren't humble.

I was reminded of this looking over the water to the store my ancestors built over a century ago. It was a two-story timber-framed building facing the wharf, still here, surviving the end of the sailing ships, the decline of the fisheries, and, more recently, rural depopulation. Ironically, we were saved by the past. With the help of Stuart Campbell, an engineer who had once gone so far as to eat ham and scalloped potatoes alone with me in my house, we now had heritage property protection for the store. This helped establish us as a tourist attraction, and that in turn drew customers for the locally produced crafts we sold on the store's second floor.

It was for those crafts, and to chat with the people who made them, that the tourists came—on bicycles, on motorcycles, in cars, buses, and vans, like the one Wally "Waldo" Butt drove. As I pulled in behind the store, I could see his van, parked crookedly and much too close to the back door.

Wally was standing at the bottom of the vehicle's steps. When he saw me, he came over, his scuffed brown shoes crunching on the gravel. I noticed he had missed a belt loop.

"A word, Valerie?" he asked, in the voice of an old friend, which he was not.

"Sure, Wally," I said, taking a step back as he moved in too close. "But can you make it fast? I understand you brought in a load of tourists. I'm here to help Rollie."

"That," said Wally with a smile, completely unaware that the long side of his comb-over had lifted straight up in the wind, "is what I wanted to talk to you about. My tours bring in a lot of business to you ladies at the Co-op." He looked around and reached out to pull me away from Darlene. "So it seems to me that it would be fair if I was duly compensated for that business."

It took me a minute. Then, I got it. "Are you asking for some kind of commission for parking your tourist van at this tourist destination? Wally, don't tell me this is a shakedown," I said, pleased with myself for sounding savvy. "Councilwoman," I called to Darlene, "do you have something to say about this?"

"Definitely," Darlene replied, as she came to stand beside me. Darlene was newly elected to the Gasper's Cove town council and was making a skilled transition from town hair stylist to local bureaucrat. "I'm interested in this little proposal, too. Something you want to put in writing, Mr. Butt?"

Wally squirmed uncomfortably, muttered something about how some people can't take a joke, and then moved toward the stairs up to the store. But before he got there, the back door banged opened, and a tall, thin woman came out.

"There you are," she shouted at Wally, marching down the steps to meet him, the waxed canvas of her brand-new vacation-in-rural-Canada barn jacket snapping as she moved. "What were you thinking?" she demanded. "Don't you know who I am?"

Wally twisted his neck inside his Nova Scotia tartan tie and snuck a look at a list in his hands. "Jennifer Fox?" he asked, unsure.

"That's me," the woman said. "The restaurant owner and food influencer. Do you know how many followers I have? Two million. And where do you take us for lunch? A drive-through fish-and-chips place. Frozen fries and frozen fish probably caught six time zones away. I am here for the authentic," she said, pointing to the words on the side of Wally's van, duct tape now covering the "Un" some local teenager had painted in front of the word *Authentic*. "I came a long way for a genuine experience."

I moved forward, nudged Wally aside, and took the woman's elbow to steer her toward the store. It was the policy at Rankin's to minimize scenes in the parking lot. "Let's go in and join the rest of your tour, Miss Fox," I said in my toddler-handling voice. "I'll show you authentic, local crafts."

Once we got our food influencer up and into the small landing inside the back door, Darlene and I made eye contact, and nodding to the stairs to the second floor, she left me to go open the cash register in the Co-op. As I watched her go, I caught a glimpse of Duck, a small gray cat pressed protectively next to his handsome Elvis Presley face. As the two of them headed down to the basement, as predicted, the famous food influencer started to tell me she had no interest in knickknacks, when Rollie stepped out of the manager's office. He put out a hand.

"Jennifer Fox?" he asked. "Welcome to Rankin's. Never forget a face. I'd recognize you anywhere." Since Rollie used one of the nation's last working flip phones and was completely indifferent to social media, I doubted this was true, but I appreciated the effort. Jennifer, it seemed, appreciated his charm.

"This is your store?" she asked brightly, rapidly rearranging her features from angry to flirtatious, as she assessed my cousin's solid frame, wild red hair and beard, and decided she was dealing with a manly man. "It's so quaint. Come here," she said, pulling Rollie toward her and simultaneously raising the phone in her right hand high above their faces. "One for my followers. Smile."

Rollie smiled, with an expression that reminded me of a young boy being told to kiss an old aunt, and then extracted himself. Behind him, his friend James Martin, visiting professor and seasonal resident, who it appeared did know who Jennifer Fox was, intervened.

15

"Miss Fox? Delighted to meet you," he said, with a sly wink at me. "We are honored, aren't we, Rollie?"

As James advanced, and Rollie retreated, I was once again impressed by the professor's social skills. No one could resist the man, not the humor in the eyes behind his rimless glasses, not the baggy corduroy pants he wore even in summer, not the shirt that was never tucked in all the way around, and not even the long lock of gray hair that routinely fell like a wing over one side of his smooth pink forehead, and which should have been annoying in anyone else, but on him wasn't.

Wally saw his chance and took it. Noting that his celebrity passenger was distracted, he slipped behind her back, out the door, and to his van and safety. I did the same, bailing on an intense discussion about chicken potpie and dashed away to see if Darlene needed help.

Upstairs, the Gasper's Crafters' Co-op was packed.

In addition to Jennifer Fox, Wally's tour had brought in several middle-aged couples who seemed to know each other and a young woman who didn't. I was gratified to see the group impressed by our everyday crafts—doormats and wreaths made from the rope used to haul up lobster traps, quilts and wall hangings made from home-sewing leftovers, hand-carved animals, knitting, and near the big half-moon window that looked out at the sea, the friendship bracelets made by young Polly and her friend Erin Campbell, Stuart's daughter.

It was a crowded space, but as I squeezed past the tourists, I caught snippets of conversation.

"This is what I came for. Do you see that stained glass?"

"Do you believe that tour guy?"

"I know. Best part was when those bird-watchers chased him off the protected lichen."

"Priceless."

"Fair Isle socks. Haven't seen those in years."

"Can't you feel the energy in this place? That's due to the intersection of the meridians."

"Meridian? I thought they called it the causeway. Or do you mean Highway Number 2?"

"You know, my mother crocheted. Do you think it's hard? Maybe when I retire."

"How about when I asked that Wally guy if the tides went in and out every day, and he didn't know?"

"And why did we have to stop all the time? What was he doing?"

"Probably asking directions. No idea where he was."

A line was forming at the counter. On my way over, I was stopped by one of the women from the tour. "What's this?" she asked, carefully holding up a beautifully carved maple stick. "It looks ceremonial."

"Depends how you look at breakfast," I said. "It's a spurtle—you know, for stirring oatmeal."

"Oh," she said, putting the wooden implement down, clearly disappointed. "I don't have breakfast. My eating window doesn't start until late afternoon."

And mine starts the minute I open my eyes and lasts till I close them at 10:00 at night, I wanted to say. "You probably wouldn't have much use for a spurtle then," I said. "Have you seen our quilted jackets?" Anyone who ate so little was bound to be cold.

"I'll check them out," she said moving over to the rack on a mission. "Thank you."

Satisfied, I walked over to the cash register. I was surprised to see Colleen behind it, helping Darlene.

I felt a tap on my shoulder.

"Excuse me? Can you help me?"

I turned around. It was the young woman from the tour. She looked almost too hip and modern for this environment in her loose rayon blouse and balloon pants, one arm tattooed entirely in vegetables, an eggplant over her elbow.

"Why are they called matinee sets? Aren't they just a cardigan, booties, and a hat?" she asked, holding up some of our knitted baby clothes.

Colleen stepped in, as this was her era of expertise. "A matinee set is sort of a dress-up outfit," she explained. "It's what you put on babies when you go out visiting in the afternoon. So they'd match."

"Match?" the young woman looked puzzled. "That's so cute. My friend's having a baby. Do you have any in gray?"

"Not sure if our older ladies do baby clothes in gray." Annette had arrived and was obviously enjoying this conversation.

"What's wrong with pink and blue?" Colleen interrupted. "Green and yellow, when you don't know what it's going to be, although now everyone does. Spoils the surprise, if you ask me."

The young woman hesitated, not sure what to say, but before I could hear the rest, Rollie came up the stairs and pulled me aside.

"Thanks for getting over here so quick," he said. "How are things over at the recycle place?"

"Going strong," I said, leaning closer; the Co-op was getting noisy as more and more visitors went up and down the stairs. "And you'll never guess what we found in the donations. A parachute from World War II! Do you believe that?"

"A parachute, you say? Where was this?" James was suddenly beside me. Nearby, Jennifer stopped at a display of church cookbooks to leaf through a copy of *Breaking Bread with Friends*, her phone down, cash in her hand.

"Across in Drummond, a spot called Recreate and Recycle Depot," I said. "We help out."

"Really? Sounds fascinating. I'll have to make a trip myself," James said. "Better yet, next time you volunteer, why don't I come with you?"

I was about to explain to Rollie's refined friend that work at the Depot involved slinging around garbage bags of odds and ends, some more odd than others, hardly what he was used to, when the loud, painful, searing sound of a car horn shattered the air.

"What in the world?" Rollie said, shouting to be heard as the noise continued without stopping. "We can't have that!"

My hands over my ears, I watched Rollie rush down the stairs, moving so quickly he bumped into a man at the bottom, probably a tourist, ridiculous in the big sun-colored sou'wester on his head. *The man in the yellow hat*, I thought to myself, *Curious George*. Startled, the man put the rain hat back on the rack, glared at Rollie, snapped on his sunglasses, pushed aside a mother with two toddlers, and stalked out the front door, followed by more customers as the unbearable noise continued. We waited one minute, two, three, five, and then, as abruptly as it had started, the horn stopped.

The entire store sighed with relief.

"At last," I said. "Darlene, I'm going to see if we can bring people back in." I ran down the stairs, but as my foot hit the old boards at the bottom, a wave of cool, alive air moved past me, like a slap. I stopped.

Someone had left the back door wide open, I walked to the rear entrance and looked out.

Rollie was in the parking lot, standing next to Wally's van at the bottom of the short flight of retractable steps, looking up and into the vehicle. His arms were spread wide like a barrier, one hand on the van's folding door, one on the handrail on the other side, as if he was trying to prevent someone from going into, or coming out of, the van.

I stepped out onto the small back landing.

"Rollie?" I called out. "Rollie?"

He didn't seem to hear me, but leaned in, closer to the interior of the van, his back a shield.

I closed the door behind me, went down the worn wooden stairs, and walked toward my cousin, the gravel of the parking lot slipping and crunching under the smooth soles of my shoes with a sound that reminded me of Wally.

Something was not right. Had I done this before? I couldn't place when.

"Rollie!" I said, but this time with urgency. "What's going on?"

Why didn't he answer me? Why wasn't he moving?

When I reached him, I put out my hand and touched Rollie's broad back.

Then, almost as if my touch hurt him, Rollie jerked and swung one hand roughly back, shoving me aside.

I stepped sideways, shocked. Rollie didn't push people.

Then, over his shoulder, I saw Duck, standing just inside the open door to the van, his head bent under the low roof.

"Duck! What's happened?" I tried to push past, but my cousin's arm again stopped me.

"Stay away, Valerie. Go inside and lock the door. Don't let anyone out here." Rollie's voice was sharp and thin. "Call the police."

"The police?"

I looked up. Duck stood in the open door. He hesitated and then walked stiffly down the stairs and onto the gravel. The sleeves of his shirt were wet and dark.

It was only then I could see into the van, the back hatch and front door still open, and see the heavy shape, slumped half in and half out of the driver's seat. The head was pulled back, and the gash on the neck was still releasing a trickle of blood that flowed down over the logo on the jacket so only the word *Authentic* still showed.

Wally "Waldo" Butt had run his last tour.

CHAPTER THREE

The two Royal Canadian Mounted Police (RCMP) cruisers from Drummond arrived in record time. Almost before the first police car stopped, Officer Wade Corkum was out and over to the van, slamming the door of his car behind him. The officer in the second car, whom I recognized as Officer Dawn Nolan, moved just as fast as she strode toward the three of us, her face grim and one hand, I noticed, on her holster. Pausing for just a moment to look at Wade, now inside the van, his voice urgent as he spoke into the microphone clipped to the top of his armored vest, Nolan ignored Rollie and me and spoke directly to Duck, who stood silently, head down, mesmerized by the dark stains on his clothes.

"You want to tell me what happened?" she said, aware as the rest of us of the blood.

Rollie stepped forward, placing himself between the officer and Duck.

"It was me. I sent Duck to see what was going on with the car alarm. He found Wally, fallen over the wheel, leaning on the horn. Duck pulled him off. That's where the blood came from," he said, eyeing Duck warily as if willing him not to speak.

"We'll decide what came from where. Step aside, sir." Nolan was curt. She called out to Wade. "They sending backup? What'd you see in there?"

Wade stepped down the van's short steps, the sunlight glinting on the edges of his shaved head under his hat. Wade and I had gone to school together. He was the kind of guy you weren't surprised to hear had gone into law enforcement but were surprised to hear he'd done well at it. It was hard sometimes to forget who someone used to be, but this was a different Wade now.

"See what the team says. The throat's been cut, no sign of a weapon, but they'll find it. A lot of blood down the back of the van. It looks like he was attacked, maybe tried to get to the front, and collapsed." Wade paused to hoist his pants up on his hips. He'd done a good job developing only his upper body with weights.

He and Nolan looked at each other and seemed to exchange some kind of RCMP code. They reached an agreement.

"Okay. Folks, I'm going to close this area off and wait for the medical examiner. Officer Nolan's going to take statements from anyone who was in the immediate vicinity Except you," he said, his face hard as he looked at Duck. "You're going to come with me. We need to hear what happened from you, in your own words. Down at the station." He glared at Rollie and pulled out his handcuffs.

Duck walked over to Wade, passing so close to me our shoulders almost touched.

"Help me," he whispered, so softly only I could hear, so quietly I wasn't sure I had.

Duck moved on, reached Wade, turned around, and put his hands behind his back, in position. He'd done this before, I realized. Wade stepped forward, and with a loud snap the handcuffs were on, and as if that were a signal, Nolan opened the back door of one of the cruisers. Then, with one large hand on Duck's forearm, Wade used the other to hold Duck's head down to guide him into the back seat.

As they drove off, Duck turned his face away from us and leaned back into the car seat. I realized he hadn't said a word to anyone once the handcuffs went on.

He'd been expecting this.

Taking our statements took most of the rest of the day. An extra officer came over from Drummond to help. I noticed how he and Nolan carefully grouped us, making sure the people on the tour were kept apart, as if preempting any possibility that they would cook up the same stories, although I wasn't sure why, since everyone was clearly upstairs at the Co-op when Wally had been killed. But my dog, Toby, and I watched a lot of police series. I knew the tricks and understood the protocols.

Nolan commandeered my sewing classroom at the front of the store for her interviews. The other officer took over Rollie's office. When it was my turn, Nolan called me into my own workspace. I was taken aback to see her in my chair, behind my beautiful old sewing machine, but, I understood, we weren't there to sew.

Nolan turned on a recorder and laid it on my sewing table, between us.

"How long have you known Wally Butt?" she began.

"Not too long," I explained. "Maybe since the beginning of the tourist season when he showed up with his van. He'd drop by and bring people to the Crafters' Co-op to shop." I left out the part about Wally being a phony and a fabricator. That didn't seem necessary. I'd seen the blood. Wally now had more than enough other troubles.

Officer Nolan took notes as we talked, comments to herself, I supposed. She watched me intently, her curly fair hair a contrast to the masculine uniform she wore, incompatible with her full, female figure. She moved on.

"Is there anything you can tell me about Wally's background?" she asked.

I hesitated, taking a moment to separate facts from the more colorful speculation that had circulated in the community.

"I can tell you this for sure," I said. "He told us he was brought up in Mississauga, you know, in Toronto, and his family were Butts from Newfoundland. A common name there," I added unnecessarily. "Guess he always figured that seawater was somehow still in his veins, though if you ask me, it was pretty diluted. He knew zero about this part of the country—he made up what he thought tourists wanted to hear. Pirates and secret coves, stuff like that."

Nolan stopped writing her notes and looked up at me. "Are you saying Wally was not honest?"

No need to think about that one. "That's exactly what I'm saying. Next question?"

"For the moment, that seems enough about Wally. What can you tell me about Duck MacDonald?"

I had to be careful here. Some of what I knew I wasn't supposed to know, but then again, I wouldn't be telling this police officer something she couldn't find out herself.

"You know Rollie worked at the prison, right? Before coming here? As a counselor?" Nolan nodded—of course she knew this, everybody did.

"Well, when he came back here, he sort of brought Duck with him. Guess Duck was in prison when Rollie was there. But I don't think it was Duck's fault he went to jail."

Nolan sat up straighter. This interested her. "Now, why do you say that?"

Where should I start?

"Listen, Duck didn't come from the most reputable family. He's one of *those* MacDonalds." I caught the look of confusion on Nolan's face and then remembered she wasn't from here. "You know, from the hills. The no-good branch of the MacDonalds."

"So," Nolan said evenly, "you're saying that Duck is," she looked down at her notes, "a no-good, too?"

Oh boy, I'd done this wrong. "No, no, that's not what I mean at all," I said, too quickly. "He grew up in that family. Dad and uncles always in trouble, up to something. If there was a crime around here, they'd say dig deep enough, and there will be a MacDonald from the hills at the bottom of it."

Nolan was writing again. "In your assessment, Duck MacDonald was raised to be a criminal?"

She was rushing the story; she didn't get it.

"Maybe, but that wasn't who he was. The MacDonald brothers were into petty shakedowns. They started

blackmailing people when they were in grade school—
you know, pay me or I'll beat you up. But when they were
older, they branched out. Duck wasn't like that at all. He
had enough trouble with school without trying to figure
out crime. Not at all like his brothers. They were naturals;
they're the ones who got him arrested."

"Is that a fact?" Nolan looked skeptical.

"Look it up." Was that the right thing to say to a police
officer? Probably not. "Guess a couple of his brothers were
counterfeiting in Montreal. Printing money. They gave
some to Duck and said, go spend it."

"Didn't he find that suspicious?" Nolan asked.

"You don't understand Duck," I tried to explain. "If you
say something, he believes it. He has trouble doing anything
else." It was time I wrapped this story up and got to the
important part, the part that would explain to this curly-
haired, sternly dressed RCMP officer who Duck really was.
"The thing is, those dummy brothers of his put the same
serial numbers on all the bills. So easy to spot, so easy for
Duck to get caught. And he did."

Nolan was interested again and started writing. Was this
good or not?

"Anyway, the judge must have figured this out," I said.
"That's why Duck is here working for Rollie, and his brothers
are still in jail."

"Hmm," Nolan was distracted. She was thinking about
something I said, but I didn't know what. "Okay, what
about Duck's relationship with Wally? Anything to say
about that?"

I thought a minute. I knew I should say that when Wally
nearly ran over Shadow, the store cat, Duck said he wanted

to kill him, but I didn't think that would be helpful. We all often feel that way about something from time to time.

"Duck avoided Wally ever since there was almost an accident in the parking lot," I said. This was true enough. "He loves that cat. So, I'd say he and Wally had no relationship at all." There, I'd fixed it.

Nolan looked bewildered again. "A cat?"

"Yes, a cat. That's everything you need to know about Duck," I explained. I believed how a person related to animals showed you who they were. "Someone brought in a bag of kittens they found beside the highway. Can you imagine people would do something like that?" I asked, but I could see right away this RCMP officer could. "Anyway, all the kittens had takers but this scraggly little gray one we didn't think would make it. Duck said no, that's the best one, and decided Shadow should live with us in the store."

Nolan looked at me for a long time, her face serious over the spool of turquoise thread on the top of the sewing machine.

"I think that's all I need for now, Ms. Rankin, as far as your witness statement goes. You've been very helpful. Maybe even more than you know."

I made a move to get up, and Nolan held up her hand. "Before you go, there is something else I have to say to you."

I sat back in my chair and waited. "What would that be?" I asked.

"I have only been in this community a short time, but you know the one thing I learned?" I shook my head. "Everyone here is related. Everyone, but maybe me. That has given you all the idea that anything that happens is your personal business. You have no boundaries at all."

I started to object but then realized she was exactly right about us.

"In a sense, we were lucky here today in terms of the investigation. Everyone was upstairs in the Co-op when Wally was found. Everyone knows he died but not the details. Only three people saw what went on. You, Rollie, and, of course, Duck. I need you to keep what you saw, and particularly what you might be thinking, to yourself. Let us do our job. Wait for the official statement. The last thing we need right now is 1,400 calls from busybodies and amateur detectives who don't know what they are talking about consuming our detachment's already strained resources."

"Do you mean me?" I asked. I had hoped Nolan had forgotten my interference in her last murder investigation. I guess she hadn't.

"Of course I mean you," Officer Nolan was firm, no hint of sympathy or humor in her voice. "Don't say anything about what you saw to anyone for the time being. Just go about your business and let us go about ours. Is that clear?"

Aware I was in trouble for something I had intended to do, but hadn't had the chance to do yet, I nodded, wondering, as I was sure Nolan did, just how long my silence would last.

CHAPTER FOUR

After Officer Nolan left, I sat alone in the familiar room, where up to now I hadn't considered anything more serious than bumpy sleeve caps, and tried to process the ugly reality that had just happened. One minute, I had been ringing up knitted baby clothes upstairs, and Duck and the cat were hiding from an obnoxious tour director in the basement. Now, on the same day, I'd been interrogated in my sewing classroom, and our gentle handyman had been whisked away in a police cruiser.

Had they taken him down to the station because he was a suspect? I understood it didn't look good, the way they'd found him, but could the RCMP, even Wade, seriously think Duck had murdered Wally? My brain could hardly stretch wide enough to hold that idea. How was it that life could do this, flip everything over in a minute without warning?

There was also the thought I was avoiding. What had Duck meant when he asked for my help? Why me? Why not Rollie, who was standing right there, with so much more education than I had, so much more experience with the justice system? What did Duck think I could do that Rollie couldn't? Me? I could make little kids laugh, turn the heel on a knitted sock, and sew pants that fit—those things I knew I could do—but what was I supposed to do for someone who had been taken away by the Mounties, wearing a bloody shirt? I was the last person to be relied on to figure something like that out.

The room felt warm. I took off my navy cardigan, and when I did, the heavy phone in my pocket banged against the back of the folding classroom chair. It buzzed with another text and I unlocked the screen, trying to reconnect with my life before the tragedy.

Hey, Mom. Coming to town tonight. Surf trip.
You around?

My heart went tight in my chest. My youngest son, Paul. Why was he coming here? To surf? Really? Didn't he have law school classes at NYU?

This is a nice surprise.

I tapped back. I was thrilled, but knew to be cool. I wouldn't ask any questions now.

Are you coming over?

Say, 5:00? Excited to see U

Me too. Take your time. I'll be around.
I'm easy.

I wrote, finishing my lying. I decided not to sign off with a heart. Too much.

My mind was racing, happy to think of something other than the events of the day. 5:00? That meant dinner. I'd have to get home to change the sheets, clean the bathroom, and cook. Tuna casserole. Paul loved it. It would be fast. He would be so happy if I had one ready. A memory of a gangly teenager standing at the open fridge, a spoon in his hand, wolfing down the casserole flashed through my mind. I didn't have much time.

I opened the door to the classroom. Officer Nolan was deep in conference with the other officer at the front of the store.

"Can I go now? I had something come up I have to do."

Nolan hesitated and then made up her mind. "Yes, sure. If we need to talk to you again, we know where to find you." She smiled as she said this, her best police joke, told to make her colleague laugh.

Grabbing my cardigan and pulling my car keys out of my purse, I ran out the front door of the store to my car, parked in one of our diagonal parking spaces on Front Street. I was thankful Darlene and I had not parked in the back lot. That was now cordoned off as a crime scene, and I had no time to waste.

Once in the car, I fastened my seat belt and started to back up. My phone rang. Maybe it was Paul.

It wasn't; it was Stuart Campbell. Some days, I felt there was a spark between Stuart and me, and other times, I thought I was imagining it, confusing friendliness with interest, humor with flirting. I was so romantically rusty that I wasn't sure I could read the signs anymore.

An out-of-the-blue call from Stuart intrigued me, but I didn't have time to talk.

"Hello, Stuart, what can I do for you?" I asked, eyeing the clock on the dashboard. If I kept moving, I could get up the hill to the house, put on the noodles for the casserole, and start vacuuming.

"Hi, Valerie, a client just told me about what happened to the tour guy, that they found him dead, right at the store, unbelievable. He wasn't that old. Thought I'd call. See if you were okay."

"Me? I'm fine," I said, realizing no one had any reason to think Wally's death was anything but natural. "The RCMP were here, they'll figure it out." I wanted to share some of my shock and worry with Stuart, but Nolan's warning to keep it all to myself was fresh in my mind. "Sorry, I'm in a hurry here. Anything else? Is Erin okay?

"Erin's fine." There was a long pause and for a moment I thought Stuart had hung up. "Listen, I was going to call anyway even before I heard the news," he said, finally. "There's one other thing. It's about the Chamber of Commerce."

The Chamber of Commerce? I had a casserole to make at home.

"Excuse me? Is this something we can talk about later?"

I heard Stuart take in a big breath and release it slowly, like a sigh. "It's about tonight. There's a dinner and dance deal. I got a spare ticket. I wondered, as someone in the community, if you might want to go?"

A spare ticket? Tonight? My son was coming home. What if Paul wanted to do something together? I hadn't seen him for months and wanted to make the most of this visit.

"Oh, Stuart. Give the ticket to someone else. Appreciate you thinking of me, but I've got something going on," I looked in the rearview mirror and eased into the street. "Nice talking to you. Say hi to Erin for me."

Released, I tore up the hill to the house and thought about Paul. Was surfing the real reason for this trip? My mind skidded around with the possibilities. School? One day, he'd be a fine lawyer, financially secure, not like his mother. Would a good job here bring him home? Was I foolish to hope for that?

Last Christmas! I remembered. When all the kids were back, we'd driven around, looking at the lights. Paul said he could see himself living near the ocean one day. Was that it? Was he coming home after he graduated? To stay?

As soon as I was home, I sprinted to the front door and let Toby, into the backyard. I watched him patrol along the edges of the fence and then sit down to survey his kingdom. With him settled, I moved quickly down the hall to the spare room to change the sheets. How nice it would be to have at least one of my children close. My daughter, Jill, was at grad school in Aberdeen, Scotland. She had a boyfriend there. My oldest boy, Matt, worked in investments in Toronto. Neither of them would ever come back to Nova Scotia to live, I knew that. But maybe Paul would. I felt something I hadn't felt in a long time.

I felt lucky.

Savoring the feeling, I went to the kitchen, let in Toby, and started to cook. I heard the front door open.

"Mom, you home?"

It was Paul. Together, Toby and I raced to the vestibule. There he was, my youngest child. So much taller than I was, with light brown curly hair like his dad, my ex-husband, but with my eyes, the Rankin eyes, one brown and one green, that special thing we had in common.

"Yo, Momma. You look good." Paul stopped to roughhouse with Toby, and the big golden retriever's tail wagged so wildly, the big dog fell over.

"So happy to see you, such a great surprise," I said. "Where are your bags? You must be hungry."

Paul walked past me and sat on the couch.

"Yeah? What do you have?"

"Tuna casserole," I'd scrambled but gotten it made, just out of the oven.

"Mom, you didn't need to do that. I don't eat tuna anymore. Too much mercury," Paul was brisk. "Had some chelation therapy in New York. You know, to clear the heavy metals from my blood."

"Oh, okay, but what are you going to eat?" I asked, going through the contents of my fridge in my head.

"Don't worry about it, I'll get something later. Can't stay long."

"What do you mean?"

"I'm meeting up with Noah. We've been talking about this for a couple of weeks. Got a friend who wanted to come to Nova Scotia to surf." Paul avoided my eyes. "So, I figured, why not? We'll crash down at Noah's place on the point, then cruise up the coast for a bit."

Noah Dixon was the young reporter I knew from the radio station CKGC. I considered Noah one of my friends, but then I remembered he and Paul knew each other through surfing.

"Got it," I said, as casually as I could. "How's school? You must be excited. Nearly done. What's next?" It didn't matter if he wasn't staying over, not if he was moving back to open his practice.

"Mom, that's something I want to talk to you about before my friend gets here. She shouldn't be long." My son took a deep breath. I had a feeling he'd rehearsed what was coming next.

"She? A girl? Your friend's a girl?" This was it, I thought. He'd come to tell me he was getting married. I was going to meet her. Were they thinking this summer? What would I wear? Darlene would have ideas. I'd have to make something new.

"Yes, Mom, a girl. Her name is Sydney Flynn. She's chill," Paul hesitated, "but would you mind getting that look off your face? This isn't about Sydney, it's about me."

I sat up straighter in Toby's favorite chair. "Go on, you can tell me anything," I said, disappointed I wouldn't be sewing a new dress. I'd been thinking silk. Dupioni.

"It's school, Mom. I'm quitting. You have no idea how boring law is," Paul said, stroking Toby's soft head, as if for support. "But the good news is, I've found my passion, what I want to do with my life. I found what makes me happy, really happy."

"That sounds good," I said. What did he mean? Business, like his brother? Veterinary medicine, like his sister?

"Pastry. Mom, I'm going to quit law school and become a pastry chef." Paul sat back on my aunt's nubby avocado green couch, relieved, and, to my surprise, proud.

Was he crazy? This was his last year. Did he have any idea how hard it was to support yourself—or, like me, three children—without a profession, without a good job?

"Sydney got me into it; she works at the most amazing restaurant. It was her idea. I'm going to stay in New York and apprentice."

For once in my life, I didn't know what to say, but I knew it didn't matter. Paul had that determined look, the one I'd first seen on his face in kindergarten.

We both sat in silence and then, almost on cue, my front doorbell rang. Awkwardly, I got up and went to the door. It was the girl from the tour, the one with the baggy pants and the eggplant on her elbow. The girl who wanted to buy gray baby clothes. And now, I realized, the reason my son the almost-lawyer-in-maybe-this-town was about to become a minimum-wage pastry chef in New York City.

I opened the door wide.

"You must be Sydney. I'm Paul's mom. Why don't you come in?"

CHAPTER FIVE

"I know who you are, from the Co-op," Sydney said. She hesitated, searching for something to say next. "Paul's here, isn't he?"

"Sure am," Paul said from behind me, moving forward to put an arm around the girl. "Come in and see the house. It's a blast from the past."

I followed the two of them into the living room and watched Sydney's reaction to the time capsule I had inherited.

"I don't believe this place," she said, taking in the high maple coffee table, the sculpted pile of the green couch, the matching armchairs, the pole lamp, and the framed sailing ship over the mantle. "How long did it take you to collect this stuff?"

"I didn't collect it, this was my aunt's house. She lives in Florida now. It's more preserved than collected," I explained. "There's even a bathroom with pink fixtures and a red Formica table and chair set in the kitchen. It all looks exactly as it did when I was a kid."

"Hey, Mom, where's the world's largest salt-and-pepper shaker collection?" Paul asked, turning to Sydney. "My great-aunt had hundreds of them all over the place, real vintage stuff. I used to play with them when we visited."

I remembered.

"They're about the only thing I've let go so far," I said. "Catherine down at the library has them on display. She says they bring in the summer residents, giving her a chance to sign them up for library cards."

Sydney smiled and walked over to look at family pictures. Toby followed her, sniffing the girl's legs more vigorously than was polite. She didn't seem to mind.

"He must smell my cats," she said. "I have two of them; they're staying with my sister."

Cats, sisters, I wanted to know more, but before I could start asking questions, Paul intervened. "We should go, Mom, down to Noah's," he said quickly. "The three of us are heading out tomorrow to catch some waves."

I'd only seen him for a minute.

"How about tea? At least have tea before you leave," I said.

Paul turned to Sydney, and when she nodded, he smiled at me. "Tea would be great, Mom, if it's not too much trouble."

"Not a problem," I said. "Sydney, come see the kitchen. The stove and fridge are the originals."

Once seated at the tiny chrome-edged table, I used the opening of Sydney's interest in my tea biscuits as an opportunity to begin some light interrogation.

"Paul tells me you are a cook," I began, careful not to mention her vegetable-covered arm.

"Yes, that's right. I was trained as a videographer, but I always loved restaurants," she said. "I started doing small plates, then moved to a milk bar in the Village."

Milk bar? That seemed like a contradiction in terms to me. "Tell me about that," I asked. I should travel one day.

Paul answered for her. "Syd worked out the most amazing recipe for cereal milk, it's one of her bestsellers with the morning crowd. You should taste it."

"Cereal milk?"

"Yeah, Mom, you know, the milk that gets left at the bottom of a bowl of cereal? It's a nostalgia thing. Remember how you used to yell at us when we had cereal and didn't finish the milk?" He smirked at me, and I saw that one dimple. "New Yorkers will pay twenty bucks a glass to recapture that experience."

And how much would they pay for a plate of good old casserole, I wondered. But before I could ask, Paul looked past me to the kitchen window, and his eyes widened.

"Mom, is that a security camera? Why do you need something like that in Gasper's Cove?"

I laughed. "It's not what you think. I have a blue jay nest out there over the back door. Duck put it up for me so I could watch them. See here," I said, picking up my phone from the counter and leaning across to show them as I scrolled through pictures. "Here are the four eggs. See how speckled they are? And here's the mom sitting on them—she didn't move for two weeks. And look here," I said, flicking to the next picture, getting excited. "This is how they looked when they were born, like miniature featherless tiny dinosaurs, their heads all tucked in."

"That's so amazing." Sydney moved closer, fascinated. "No feathers?"

"They're coming now," I said, scrolling ahead, showing her the same chicks a few days later, skin green and bumpy, and then yesterday, the beginnings of blue quills pushing out through their tiny wings. "I get up every morning and check them. I have an alert Duck put on my phone so I know when there is movement, usually when the mom goes away, and I can take a picture."

"I'd love it if you could share these shots," Sydney said. "I've never seen anything like this." She picked up her phone. "What's your number? I'll send you a text." She lifted her face from the screen and smiled at me.

"Syd's not just a chef," Paul said proudly. "She's also an artist. A digital artist."

"I try," Sydney said, looking at Paul, both embarrassed and pleased with the way he made sure I knew how talented she was. "This is a great setup. Who is this guy Duck?"

"Duck?" In my excitement over Paul's visit, I had briefly put the afternoon at the store out of my mind. "He works for Rollie. He can do anything, odd jobs." I took a slow breath. "He's also the poor guy who found the tour operator dead in the van." I paused with a sudden realization. "Oh my, you were on his last tour, weren't you?"

Sydney nodded, uncomfortable. "I'm afraid so. The whole thing was so strange. And I mean, who goes on a lame tour and the guy who drives ends up dead?"

"What do you mean *lame?*" I asked. "I've heard a few things about Wally's operation, but I don't know what went on."

Sydney leaned forward. "Okay. The other people on the tour were nice, except that so-called influencer. I can tell you, that woman spends very little time in a real kitchen. All she did was complain when we stopped. And we stopped a lot."

"What do you mean?" I asked, "Like at sights?"

"A few, at... what do you call lookouts around here? Look-offs?" I nodded. Every view around here was at the top of a cliff.

"Yeah, Wally would tell us some story that I am pretty sure he stole from the *Pirates of the Caribbean* movie, drive a bit, and then stop. He called them 'comfort breaks,' but honestly, usually, he was the only one who went in. It was like some weird tour of Nova Scotia gas stations. I figured the guy must have had some kind of medical problem." She looked at me. "Is that why he died?"

This was exactly what I was not supposed to share.

"Maybe," I said vaguely. "The medical examiner will figure that out. Pretty terrible introduction for you to the province."

Sydney shrugged. "Poor guy, guess it happens," she said. "I've been wanting to come here for a long time," she added smiling across the table at Paul as he stood up, ready to leave, "for the surf, you know."

"There's always lots of that," I said as I followed them to the front door. Paul turned, put out his arms, and I hugged him hard. Then, to be polite, I reached over and gave Sydney a loose hug, too, aware my son was watching me.

"See you soon, Momma," Paul said, his hand on Sydney's shoulder. "Catch you when we swing back. Love ya."

"Love you, too," I said.

Then, they were gone. Toby ran over to the couch and jumped up, his big paws hanging over the back, almost touching the windowsill, wagging his tail as the car drove away. More discretely, I went quickly to the bathroom, stepped into the bathtub, and pulled the curtain aside from the little window. My face hidden, I watched them go down the street and around the corner. They'd borrowed Noah's surfer van; I recognized the bumper stickers on the back.

When there was nothing left to see, I got out of the bathtub and joined Toby in the living room. An alert went off on my phone. The mother bird had returned to her nest. I reached for my big dog's leash and called Toby off the couch. I needed a walk, a very long walk. I had a lot to process, some thinking to do. Paul had a lightness in him I hadn't seen in a long time. That made me happy, but still, my chest hurt. It was hard when you knew what you needed to feel but felt something else instead. Plus, who in their right mind would pay twenty dollars for fake milk left at the bottom of a cereal bowl? And what was I to make of the disorganized start-and-stop tour Sydney had described in the pre-murder Authentic Celtic Tours van?

I'd eat that tuna casserole myself, later. But not until I figured some of this out. I was sure there was no real way I could help Duck, but still, I had to wonder. Something I'd read was nagging at me.

The back of the van as it headed down the hill.

The plastic bumper sticker just below the rear window.

All who wander are not lost.

I stood still, the leash in my hand, the front door open.

Was Wally "Waldo" Butt really in the tour business, or did he have another reason for cruising the Nova Scotia coast?

CHAPTER SIX

I didn't sleep well that night, as I hadn't any night in the last week, even after a long walk with Toby in the hills behind the house. I got up and looked out the window, but the clouds covered the stars. There was not one area of my life that didn't worry me. I couldn't get the image of Duck coming down the van stairs with blood on his hands out of my mind, and I couldn't retreat to my family for safety because I felt like a failure as a mother. Other women seemed to smoothly transition from mom-involved to mom-on-the-sidelines. I wasn't doing a good job of it, not at all.

There was only one thing to do—have lunch and a full-on life workshop with Darlene at the Agapi, the best Greek restaurant this side of the causeway—in fact, the only restaurant this side of the causeway.

Darlene and I had counseled each other through multiple ups and downs—in her case, three husbands, and in mine, one husband who never understood what being married meant. For most of her adult life, Darlene had been the town's hair stylist, running the business out of the basement of her bungalow on Flying Cloud Drive. But lately, and not without incident, she had been elected town councillor with a record margin of 87%. We were still trying to figure out who the 13% who hadn't voted for her were. We'd narrowed it down to three theories: (1) old girlfriends of Darlene's ex-husbands, (2) bald men who had no reason to appreciate Darlene's considerable skill in hair design, or (3) resentful relatives of the former town warden, Mack MacRae, who'd left office after being pushed off his boat and into the propeller, an event that had nothing to do with Darlene and a lot to do with his own wife, Maureen.

I'd never tell her this, but I had even considered not voting for Darlene myself, despite the sign on my lawn. I knew she could do the job, but part of me was afraid that if Darlene went into politics, she'd leave me behind.

I shouldn't have worried.

Darlene was still the same, just now out of the basement and behind a desk at the town office. Like always, we discussed everything with each other, except maybe the council's budget, which was fine with me because I hated numbers, and we continued to eat lunch at the Agapi.

A local landmark, the Agapi had been opened by Nick Kosoulas and his wife, Sophia, soon after they had arrived thirty-five years ago from Greece. They still ran it themselves, with their son, George, a charming man who was doing his best, with little success, to take over the business from his father.

The food at the Agapi was wonderful. Nick's roast lamb was exceptional, and the particular blend of spices he used was a secret he shared with no one—not his wife and not his son. I felt this worried George for future-of-the-business reasons but doubted Sophia cared. Her specialty was baking, and her baklava had eased me through many life crises.

Today, Darlene was at the restaurant before me, already in a booth, her hair smooth and straightened, a navy jacket covering her scoop-neck turquoise knit top. The restaurant was busy with tourists, a few I recognized from Wally's tour the day before, and some locals. But even the noise of cutlery clinking plates, laughter, and chatter didn't drown out the noise of an argument coming through the opening from the kitchen.

"You can't keep firing dishwashers. What are we going to do?" Normally an even-tempered man, George was beside himself.

"That guy didn't know what he was doing," Nick's voice rose. "Spots. I had to redo everything myself."

"Dad, I'm telling you, it's not his fault. Stop trying to fix the dishwasher yourself. We can get a new one. It's time to upgrade, or get someone to fix it."

"Fix it? By who? That criminal Duck MacDonald? Or upgrade? Like you want to replace me? Is that it?"

George knew customers were listening. "We have orders, Dad, so why don't you go out front and take over the cash from Mom? Cool off."

"I don't need any cooling off," Nick said as he came through the swinging kitchen door and into the restaurant. "Sophia, I'll take over. You go in and help our genius son."

Sophia looked at Nick calmly—she'd learned to not let anything disrupt her serenity years ago—and stepped out to make room for her husband behind the counter. "That Greek newspaper you've been waiting for is here, under the counter."

"Good," Nick said. "Something intelligent to read."

With a small smile on her face, Sophia walked to our booth and stopped to say hello.

"Sophia, my emotional support baker," I said. "How are you?"

"Good, good," she reached over and patted my hand. "I see you have your lawyer boy here now. I'll send some baklava home for him," she said, taking our order and then mercifully moving away from the table before I was compelled to explain Paul's decision to return not to the law but to cereal milk in New York City.

I turned to Darlene. We had to get started.

"I know," she said holding up a palm. "Before we get into what happened to Wally, I have to tell you something. Paul and Sydney dropped by my place before they went to your house. He was worried about how you'd react when he told you he was quitting school." She looked down at her place setting and rearranged the cutlery. "I told him you would be fine, that you'd understand."

"He saw you before he saw me?" I asked, hurt. "Why did you tell him I'd be fine? I am not; you know I'm not. I'm a wreck."

"I lied," Darlene shrugged. "It seemed like the best thing to do. Besides, it's how you have to handle this. His mind is made up. You have no choice."

"But he had a secure future ahead of him, one less for me to worry about."

Darlene stared at me. "You have no one to worry about. Your history isn't Paul's. You struggled, but you can't lay that on him. Better a happy pastry chef than an unhappy lawyer."

Darlene was right, and I knew it. As usual, she wasn't letting me feel sorry for myself. She never did.

The first course of the food arrived. Darlene tore off a piece of pita and dragged it through the perfect, garlicky, rich tzatziki. She studied my face, as if assessing the chances that I was about to lie to her.

"So, yesterday, you spent a lot of time in the classroom with Officer Nolan after they found Wally. What was that about?" she asked, looking down as she reached for another piece of pita, giving me some time to put together an answer.

"Oh, just general stuff," I answered. "How I knew Wally." I hesitated, unsure of how to tell Darlene the truth while keeping my promise to Officer Nolan.

We moved back to let Sophia put more plates on the table. Darlene carefully pulled Nick's amazing lamb from the bamboo skewers with her fork while she thought.

"Okay, I guess, but I don't understand why they took Duck in. Maybe because of his record. That man has nothing but bad luck. You know the story, don't you? Why he went to jail?"

"Of course," I said. "It was Mr. Kosoulas who caught the bills and turned him in. Rollie says that's why Duck is too ashamed to come in here. The store brings in propane for the stove, but Duck won't deliver it until after hours."

"Exactly," said Darlene. "Can you blame him?" She stopped eating and looked straight at me. "Something's up, isn't it? Rollie's been over with the RCMP all morning, Polly told me. Why would he be doing that?"

"No idea, you'd have to ask him," I answered, desperate to change the subject before I told Darlene everything. It didn't feel right not to tell her. "So, what have you been up to?" I asked.

Darlene sighed. She knew me. "The usual stuff. Updos for prom. Council meetings." Darlene had her councillor's face on. "Mounties have been talking to us, too. Asked us to watch for unusual activity along the coast, whatever that means. That's been going on since the rumrunner days, you know that. I've got other things to worry about. We're going to replace the water lines on Front Street. Rate payers won't be too happy about that."

She stopped eating. "Speaking of engineering projects, who do you think I saw at the Chamber of Commerce dinner and dance?" she asked.

"No idea," I said, knowing exactly what she was going to say next.

"Mr. Stuart Campbell, having a few turns around the dance floor with that youngish accountant doing the audit." Darlene moved on to her Greek salad and looked at me intently over the tops of her cat-eye glasses.

"Young accountant?" I asked with an exaggerated casualness that would fool no one, least of all Darlene. "What's she like?"

"Hmm. I'd describe her as a very precise sort of person. Someone you would trust with your taxes. But cute. Perky."

There you go, I thought. No one would ever accuse me of too much precision, or trust me with their taxes, and no one called a size sixteen, forty-eight-year-old woman perky. So, that was Stuart's type. Good to know.

Darlene impaled an olive. "I think you should consider making yourself more emotionally available."

"What does that mean? You're sounding like some self-help book. I'm as available as I have time to be."

"My point exactly."

"Stop it. I'm fine the way I am. As for Stuart, good for him, a perky accountant and a clueless man. They sound ideal for each other," I said. "Let's have some baklava."

Inside, I was mortified. As I sat and waited on the red vinyl upholstery of the booth for my emergency dessert, I stewed. Me, unavailable? I knew lots of people; I talked to people all the time. I talked to dog walkers, to women who needed help putting in zippers, to men who carved little wooden animals, to mitt knitters, and to earring makers. I had Rollie and Duck, even though Duck was currently in police custody, and Darlene, my sewing students, and the people in the Crafters' Co-op. I had Kenny, who knew about birds and the building code. I had Annette, who worked in Recreate and Recycle and sold me Tupperware, and I had Catherine from the library. I had three children, and one of them was even in the same province right now. I was related by blood or marriage to more than half of Gasper's Cove, population 2,200. I considered myself multigenerationally approachable and as proof was on very good terms with two girls who were teenagers: Polly, who hung around the store and tried to manage it, and Stuart's daughter, Erin, my best junior crafter. I was completely approachable and available. Stuart could see that. I opened my mouth to share this with Darlene, but before I could, we were interrupted by the now-familiar loud voice of Jennifer Fox, standing at the restaurant's cash register.

"I don't have all day for this," she said to Nick. "I have been here for thirty-four minutes, and no one has even taken my order. You can't run a restaurant like this."

"Are you telling me how to run a restaurant?" Nick said, working himself up to the level of his dishwasher-firing fury. "What do you know about food?"

"What do I know about food?" Jennifer said, her level of indignation rising to match Nick's like the arrow on a competing blood pressure cuff. "Do you know who I am? I am trained in classic cuisine."

"Classic?" Nick shouted. "You want to see classic?" He pulled out the newspaper Sophia had stowed away from him under the counter. "Look at this. The picture of this ring. The Greek Minister of Culture is coming to Canada because they found this ring in some actor's collection. Three thousand years old, stolen from the museum in Rhodes. They're taking it back to Greece, where it belongs. Three thousand years. That's experience. That's culture, not some person who thinks half an hour is too long to wait to eat food."

Jennifer Fox whipped her phone out of her pocket and began tapping. "No one talks to me like that, no one. I'm reviewing you. *'So much for Nova Scotia hospitality. I assume the Agapi restaurant serves food, but I wouldn't know. All this establishment seems to serve up is poor service, arguments in the kitchen, and rude staff. Avoid at all costs.'*"

Jennifer looked up at Nick with triumph, revenge, and vindication on her face. "There, I just posted. What do you say now?"

"What I say is this," Nick said, snatching the cell phone from Jennifer's manicured hand and holding it high. "I can stop your stupid review." He let go of the phone and we watched, mesmerized, as it fell into the fish tank at one end of the long counter, bounced off a fake china castle, scared the angelfish, and settled into the multicolored beads, stones, and sand at the bottom of the tank, like a tiny, high-tech submarine.

"There," Nick said. "I deleted it."

CHAPTER SEVEN

George Kosoulas rushed over to the counter.

"Dad, are you crazy?" he shouted. He turned to Jennifer. "I am so sorry, Ms. Fox. My father is proud of what he does, and he has no idea how the Internet works. We'll pay for a new phone." He shot a look at Nick before the older man could interrupt. "In the meantime, would you please let us serve you lunch, on the house?" His large, dark eyes pleaded with Jennifer for understanding. He reached over to a stack of glossy calendars on the counter. "Here, please, take one of these, I took the photos myself."

I watched, fascinated by an expert in action. George was a good-looking man in a solid way and, in addition to taking the odd tourist out for a sail, was known to keep company with a variety of women, mainly seasonal visitors who went for rides on his boat and let him cook for them in the kitchens of rented houses until they left after Labor Day, no strings attached. George knew how to charm, that was certain, and as he leaned in closer, I saw Jennifer's outrage turn to something else, just as it had with Rollie. After a moment's hesitation, she relented and allowed herself to be led to a good table near the front window of the restaurant.

After she'd been served, George came to our table, picked up our plates, and deposited two of his mother's baklava in front of us. I looked over to where Jennifer was well into her lunch. Even from here, I could smell the aroma of lamb, marinated, and spiced—a food group all its own. "How's our cooking expert doing?" I asked.

"One step forward, one step back," George said, leaning in to whisper to us. "She's into negotiations. She says if Dad gives her the recipe for the lamb, she'll forget the phone. I'm not even going to ask him, he'll kill me. And her."

I started to laugh but stopped when the door to the restaurant opened. Rollie walked in with a look on his face I hadn't seen since our grandfather's funeral. Something had happened.

He walked quickly over to our booth and, nodding to George, slid in beside me, facing Darlene.

"I've just met with Officers Corkum and Nolan," Rollie said. "I have news. They're charging Duck with Wally's death. They found the murder weapon, a knife, when they searched the store. It was in Duck's old hockey jacket, hanging out back. It doesn't look good."

"What?" Darlene and I said together.

"That's impossible," I said.

Rollie held up a hand before I could go any further. "Stay out of it. I can tell you from experience, the best thing to do is let the RCMP do their job. Then, it will be up to the courts."

A knowing look crossed Darlene's face. "But it doesn't look good, does it?" she said. "He's done time already, and now they found the murder weapon. What do you expect them to think?"

"Don't get ahead of yourself," I snapped. "That was a long time ago. He's not like that, is he, Rollie?"

"I wouldn't think so," my cousin said. "But he's been in some trouble since he got out. Violence charges made and withdrawn. I learned that today. A run-in with a property owner. And there's Duck himself."

I didn't like the sound of this. "What do you mean?" I asked. There was something odd and flat about Rollie's tone. I'd expect him to be more upset, to sound more like he cared.

"According to Officer Nolan, when they took him in, he said to her, 'Only a matter of time.'" Rollie sighed. "He hasn't said anything else since."

"Once a MacDonald, always a MacDonald, maybe he meant that," Darlene said. "It's a lot to overcome."

I stood up. I needed fresh air. I put a bill on the table and reached for my jacket.

Rollie put out a hand and laid it on my arm.

"Listen, Val. I understand how you feel, and I know you get caught up in things. But I understand more about the justice system than you do. If Duck is innocent, and I hope he is, they will find that out. Any messing around you do will just get in the way of that." Rollie studied me. "You need something to take your mind off this. Come to think of it, I need a favor."

"What's that?" I asked, hearing the lack of enthusiasm in my own voice.

Rollie looked pleased to think he'd distracted me. "It's Shadow, the cat. Can you go by Duck's place and get her food? She hasn't eaten anything since he's been gone. Polly says he gets something special ordered in and keeps it at home."

"That's cats," said Darlene, watching me closely. Darlene knew her cats, whom she considered more reliable and interesting than any of her husbands. "They know what they like. You better get her what she wants."

"I'll see what I can do," I said, perking up, not, as they thought, because I had an errand, but because I realized this mission would give me access to Duck's apartment. Who knew what I might find there?

"But how am I supposed to get in?"

"Here," Rollie said, reaching into the pocket of his pleated khaki pants and pulling out a huge ring of keys. "These are Duck's—he left them in the office. His car and house keys are on it. Go around to his building on Dominion Avenue. If you run into the police, tell them to call me. I'll explain about the cat food."

I took the keys and saw the relief on Rollie's face.

"Okay, I'll go do this for the poor cat," I said. "Of course I will. But I have to say, I'm surprised at you, Rollie, and you, too, Darlene. You both seem to be just accepting that Duck might be charged with murder. No one ever stands up for Duck or people like him or listens to them. You two don't know what that feels like." Rollie and Darlene exchanged a concerned look, and that annoyed me. I remembered Duck's face as he passed me on the way to the police cruiser yesterday. I took a breath.

"I'm going to do something."

Rollie stared at me. "Like what?"

"Think. Have you seen the bags Duck makes out of sails? I know that man. He can sew," I said, as if that explained everything. "There has to be another side to this." I leaned down to the table to scrape the last few honey crumbs from my plate before I left. "And I am going to find out what that is."

CHAPTER EIGHT

And so I left, heading down Front Street toward to the corner of Dominion, leaving Rollie and Darlene behind in the restaurant.

As I walked, the heavy key ring in my pocket banged against my thigh, a solemn reminder of my mission to retrieve food for a hungry cat and to learn more about the man who had asked for my help.

Ahead of me on the sidewalk, I saw a pair of joggers, maybe a block away, coming toward me. One of them, a woman, ran on her toes, with her heels never touching the ground. As she bopped toward me, lithe and purposeful, the ponytail under the back of her baseball cap swinging back and forth like a shiny pendulum, I saw how fit she was. I could see a taut, ridged abdomen between her short, tight jogging shorts and a sports bra. As the couple was about to pass me, I realized I knew the other runner.

Stuart.

Here he was, on my side of the water, jogging in the middle of a workday. He was not, I noticed, running on his tippy-toes, and I was certain I could hear the slap, slap of wide feet on the pavement as he neared me, in his black work socks, faded shorts, and an old T-shirt covered in the holes of fabric rot.

So, Stuart was jogging. This ballerina must be the accountant Darlene had told me about. She certainly looked perky and youngish.

"Hello, Stuart," I said in my best couldn't-care-less voice. Why did I never follow Darlene's never-leave-the-house-without-lipstick rule? "I didn't know you ran."

Stuart stopped, sneaking in an excuse to catch his breath.

"Yeah, I did track in high school," he said and then looked sideways at his partner, as if wishing he could take the words back. "Getting back into it."

I didn't think the dancing accountant heard him. Impatient, she jogged on the spot, not wanting to waste any steps, and pulled a tube from behind, stuck it in her mouth, and took a long suck. A backpack of water.

"I'm sorry," Stuart said, remembering his manners. "This is Kimberly. We're working on a few things together at the Chamber of Commerce."

Kimberly gave Stuart an amused look and continued to bob.

Soldiering on, Stuart continued, as if trying to make up the ground he'd just lost. "I've been meaning to reach out to you," he said.

Reach out? Stuart sounded like a millennial real estate agent trying to sell a condo, and not like a middle-aged consulting engineer in old shorts and black socks.

"Really? What about?" I asked. Not dinner-and-dance dates—that ship had, apparently, sailed.

"I was at the library with Erin. Chatted with Catherine. She showed me that parachute. I think I know where it's from," he said, rushing his words as the runner beside him double-timed her bouncing. "Now's not the time, but maybe I can come into the store. I have something to show you."

"Sure, anytime," I said. Let's keep it formal. "I never go anywhere," I added, and regretted it.

The girl reached for her feeding tube again, and this time, after taking a drink, she handed it to Stuart. With an awkward look at me, he took a quick sip and gave it back. Then, with a wave, he followed his jogging buddy down the path. Watching them go, I decided they looked like a pair of toddlers, sharing a pacifier. The mean thought surprised me. I had no time for that; I was a big girl, with real work to do.

Gasper's Cove was so beautiful, I didn't think there were any bad views in town. But Duck had managed to find one. His apartment building, down the raggedy end of the road, faced the shipping containers piled up behind the fish plant on one side and garbage bins on the other.

102 Drummond Street was a small block of a building, divided into about a dozen apartments, built to house the seasonal workers who sometimes came up and worked at the plant. No saving had been spared in the building's construction. The sides were encased in metal siding, punctured here and there by small aluminum windows, and the roof was flat.

What looked to be a small back door turned out to be the front entry. The tiny vestibule inside was decorated with a *No Fliers/Flyers* sign that no doubt kept both the junk mail and pilots out and tiny hand-written cards, some with the names crossed out, beside each apartment number.

It took me a minute to find where Duck lived until I found a "Donald MacDonald" in the basement. The first challenge was to get past the entry and into the building. I fumbled with the ring and tried to find the key that would open the inner door.

"Wrong key, hon, try the bigger one," a voice said behind me. I turned and saw a short, round, blond woman in her fifties close behind me, her arms wrapped around a Sobey's reusable grocery bag, celery leaves and the top of a bag of Covered Bridge chips escaping from the top. The shopper, clearly a resident, made encouraging noises as she watched me sort through the keys.

"Sorry," I said, "just here to water a friend's plants." I had no idea if Duck had any plants.

"That's nice of you. Not to worry, I'll let you in." The woman smiled at me and reached past to wiggle the key in the lock. "Who's your friend? You're with the RCMP, aren't you?"

Gasper's Cove. News around here traveled faster than the speed of sound.

"No, afraid not, just here for the plants," I said, hoping to avoid long conversations about dead tourist operators or store handymen. "Thanks for the door. You've been a big help." I squeezed past the tenant through the door and started down the hall.

"It's the quiet ones you have to watch," the woman called after me. I wasn't sure if she was referring to me or to Duck, but not waiting to find out, I kept going down the narrow hallway to the stairwell and the basement, feeling the woman's amused eyes on my back.

There were four apartments on the lower level. Duck's was the only one without a floral wreath, a mud tray for boots, or a sign that said "Welcome" beside the door.

I hesitated, feeling slightly guilty about violating Duck's privacy as I turned the keys around, looking for one that might open an apartment door. I decided to try one with the word *Schlage* on it because it looked like the key to my own house.

It worked, and I was in.

The apartment was just one large room with windows set just above ground level. The walls were painted a light green that matched the laminate counter that ran along one wall of the kitchenette. The furniture looked to have come to Duck secondhand from someone else. There was a polyester velveteen couch patterned in a print of orange and brown trees against one wall, a low dentist office–style coffee table, and a big screen TV. A double bed, legless and flat on the floor, was neatly made, with hospital corners in the gray wool blanket. There were no pictures on the wall.

After having lived so long with my aunt's decoration density, the lack of personal possessions in this room unsettled me. But then I turned to the kitchenette. There, on the fridge, were two photos. One was taken soon after Shadow had been rescued. My heart broke to look at it—she was so small, her fur so rough, her body so thin. By contrast, the second photo, taken more recently by Polly, I expected, showed a different animal: a cat with a shiny coat, her eyes half closed as Duck rubbed her under her chin, so content I could almost hear her purr.

This little cat was his real family, I realized, as I pulled myself away. He would want me to take good care of her. I had to find the cat food; that's why I was here. Where was it? One by one, I opened the cupboards. Inside, I found neat stacks of mismatched dishes, cans of soup and boxed macaroni, and finally, high at the top in the cupboard over the sink, I could see several rows of "Sensitivities limited ingredient grain-free pollock pâté."

I reached up and loaded the small tetra packs of cat food into the shopping bag I carried in my purse. When this was done, I stood still and rotated to look at the tiny apartment. What now? I told myself to be responsible and head out, but I didn't move toward the door. Maybe, since I was here already, a little light looking around wouldn't hurt. Who knows? I might find something that would help Duck, possibly even prove there was no reason for him to kill Wally. Who was I kidding? What would that even look like? I was just nosy.

I started with the bathroom.

Like a sneaky neighbor over for New Year's Eve, I opened my absent host's bathroom cupboard and looked. It was nearly empty—just a bottle of Tums, a tube of antibiotic cream, carefully rolled up from the bottom, and four different kinds of bandages. I was disappointed.

I moved back into the main room. On the floor beside the bed was a small stack of library books. I picked one up and read the title. Judging by the dark cover, which involved swords, serpents, and medieval scrolls, the book was some kind of historical saga. I returned it to the pile of books, which all looked to be of the same type, and then noticed the orange label on the spine: YAF Young Adult Fantasy.

Shrugging at Duck's tastes in literature, I stepped over and opened the closet. Inside, I found a neat stack of jeans and T-shirts, all folded with military precision on a shelf, and a few jackets—one for rain, one for wind, and one for snow.

Déjà vu. I'd done this before, exactly this. The realization made me feel sick.

Many years ago, when the kids were in bed and my husband once again was not at home, I searched closets for clues. I usually found them. The memory made me anxious, but, I remembered, this was how I had discovered what I needed to know. I reached out and checked the pockets in each jacket. There wasn't much there: a few Canadian Tire store and drive-through coffee receipts, a rumpled napkin, and a torn admission ticket, but in the last jacket, I found a paper, neatly folded, the creases worn as if it had been folded and unfolded many times.

I couldn't stop myself. Opening the note, I moved closer to the light of the high basement window to read.

Never forget what you did.

CHAPTER NINE

I stared at the paper and then read it again. Who wrote it? What did it mean? Duck certainly knew; the worn creases in the paper told me these words had been read over and over again.

Lost down the tunnel of my thoughts, I was startled when I heard a car door slam on the street outside. I moved to the side of the narrow window and looked out, just in time to see Wade Corkum and Dawn Nolan striding purposely up the walkway toward the building. Nolan, I noticed, had a large black case in her hand.

The pair of officers were dressed identically. Both had the characteristic yellow RCMP stripes running down the outer seam of their dark pants, and both wore short-sleeved gray shirts and black padded vests branded with the word *Police* in big white letters. The similarity ended there. Wade's shaved head was underneath his hat, and Nolan's curly blond hair was twisted up and tucked in, and she was the one with the I-mean-business look on her face. It seemed to me that if I were a criminal, Nolan would be the one who would worry me the most. As I watched Wade's broad torso march up to the door of the building with such confidence, a line from a Phyllis McGinley poem ran through my mind: "But little girls can draw conclusions, And profit from their lost illusions."[1] I suspected this might describe RCMP Officer Dawn Nolan's professional life.

Moving away from the window, I made up my mind. With the note still in my hand, I heaved my bag of premium cat food onto my shoulder and left Duck's apartment to climb the stairs to meet the two officers.

We arrived in the small entrance at the same time.

"Small world," I said, wishing I didn't use clichés when I was under pressure. "I was just in Duck's apartment, getting food for our cat. We were getting worried she'd starve to death."

Wade crossed his arms. "And how do you have a key?" he asked.

"It was here," I said holding up Duck's heavy key ring, "at the store. Rollie sent me over."

Wade relaxed slightly at Rollie's name. Apparently, my cousin had more credibility than I did.

"We will take those from you," Wade said, extending an official hand. "That apartment is now part of an ongoing investigation. We don't want anyone in there."

"Got it," I said moving aside to let Wade pass to go down the hall. Nolan started to follow, but as she came near, I put out a hand and laid it on her arm.

"Officer Nolan, if you have a minute?"

Nolan stopped, looked at me, then called out to Wade, "I'll be right with you." She turned to me and waited.

---

1. Phyllis McGinley, *A Short Walk from the Station* (The Viking Press, 1951)

I reached down and extracted the note from my pocket and handed it to her. "When I was getting the cat food, I saw this on the floor," I mumbled. I had to refine my lying skills. "I picked it up. I thought you should see it."

Slowly, and with a look that reminded me of my mother when she didn't believe a word I said, Nolan snapped on a pair of disposable gloves and pulled a small plastic bag from the kit in her hand. She carefully unfolded the note, read it, refolded it, and put it into the bag.

"Well?" I said. "This is a major clue, isn't it? This might prove Wally's death wasn't a Duck thing but some other bad guy's thing, won't it?" I was elated. I was cut out for criminal investigative work. I wondered what the age limit was for joining the RCMP.

Nolan took her time responding. "All this proves is that there are some words on a paper you found when you searched Duck's apartment, without authorization. Thanks for this," she held up the bag. "You'll hear from us. Until then, look up the penalties for interfering with an investigation. I'd hate to think someone like you would do something like that."

I opened my mouth to either apologize or explain, but before I could say anything, Nolan headed down the hall, caught up with Wade, and disappeared down the stairs to the basement.

I sighed. I had been dismissed, and now I was worried. I remembered Nolan's gloves and thought of all the things I'd touched in the apartment. I bet I'd hear from the RCMP again, and it wouldn't be from a recruiter. What had I been thinking?

Out on the street, I stood for a while, considering my ineptitude, then I remembered Shadow. Somewhere in Rankin's General, there was a small hungry cat, and here I was, holding her food. Some animal lover I was. Pulling myself into the present, I set off for the store to feed Duck's best friend, leaving Wade and Nolan behind to conduct their own professional, competent, and officially sanctioned search of his apartment.

Once at the store, I realized finding Shadow was not going to be easy. For almost half an hour, I walked up and down the aisles, a small bowl of slimy, stinky, but irresistible pollock in my hand, until I finally found her in with the cleaning supplies, next to the display of mops and brushes, deep inside a large red plastic pail. When she heard her name, the cat raised her small gray head and stared at me with large, round yellow eyes.

"Meow."

Quickly, before she could escape, I scooped Shadow up, my hands circling her soft belly. Ignoring her protests, I held her tightly to my chest and walked to the front of the store.

Polly was behind the counter, receipts spread out in piles, a laptop open in front of her.

"You just missed her," she said.

"Who?"

"That Kimberly person, the one after Erin's dad."

I kept my face neutral. "What did she want?"

"You. Get this, she said she heard you sewed and had some jeans that needed hemming. She asked if she could drop them off." Polly rolled her eyes.

I nearly choked. "What did you tell her?"

"What do you think? I said you were the CEO of a creative start-up and suggested she find a tailor over at Drummond to do it." Polly was indignant. "And I told her she should sign up for a class and learn how to do it herself. The nerve."

Kimberly was the last person I wanted to see in my classes. "Not to worry," I said, appreciating my defender. What was a start-up? Something that you were starting up, I figured, which was probably not a bad description of the Co-op. "Most people have no idea what sewing is, not her fault." I put the dish of food down on the counter and, with the cat still in my arms, looked over to see a spreadsheet on the screen. It appeared that our junior high helper was doing the Craft Co-op's books.

"How's it going?" I asked her.

Polly looked up at me and pushed her glasses up her beautiful straight nose. "Pretty good," she said. "We're up 12 percent this quarter over last, and our year-to-date doesn't look so bad. The challenge will be to hold this growth after the season ends."

Polly was always worried about the end of the tourist season. She had pushed us to set up an online store "to mitigate exposure," whatever that meant.

"But I thought we were doing quite well with the Internet sales," I said. "They bring in almost as much as the store."

Polly tapped a fluorescent-painted fingernail on the paper. "True, but we need to broaden the customer base. We have a few repeat customers, like Rollie's friend James and someone from Boston, but we need to diversify."

Shadow started to squirm in my arms, but I held on. "Can you explain what you just said?" I asked. I often wondered who the grown-up was in this relationship.

Polly leaned forward on the counter. She had chopped her long black hair off into a blunt cut, but I missed the French braids.

"Take the friendship bracelets Erin and I have on the market. They are our bread and butter. Junior high students are a highly loyal demographic, and it's year-round. But the necklaces like the ones you make, they're going out to the same few customers, all online. We need to think about sustainability."

Hearing enough about e-commerce, Shadow struggled out of my arms and jumped down onto the counter. She delicately moved her nose to the bowl and started eating.

Polly reached over and gently stroked the cat's rounded back. "What's going to happen to her now?" she asked, "Duck was her person." She looked up at me.

I wavered, then made up my mind.

"I'm going to take her home until, you know, until Duck comes back." I was unsure of what else to say.

Polly stared at me for a moment and then, too, seemed to make up her mind.

"About that," she said. "No one will tell me what's going on, but I figured it out, what happened to Wally and why Duck's not around. People think someone my age doesn't hear things, but they're wrong." She tapped on the keys in front of her, closed the window with the Craft Co-op's statements on it, and opened another one that asked for a password. She turned the laptop around so I could see the screen.

"What's this?" I asked, as a sick feeling grew in my stomach. Adult troubles shouldn't involve kids.

"Data," Polly said with pride. "Evidence. A list of all the people who didn't like Wally, besides Duck."

I was speechless, horrified Polly was even thinking like this, but still, I couldn't resist reading. The names were familiar, but in most cases, the grievances so meticulously listed were news to me:

1. Tour people. Mr. Martin said good money for a useless tour to nowhere.

2. Kenny the inspector guy. Wally wrecked a protected area.

3. Catherine at the library. Burned her Wally didn't do his research.

4. Toby. Loves everybody else. For dog reasons.

5. Darlene's mom, Colleen. Wally was in her woods. He said he was lost, she said he was snooping.

6. Shadow. Almost hit by the van. Also other cat reasons?

7. Old Mr. Kosoulas. Wally never tipped. Big mistake.

8. Lady in Drummond who rented him a cottage. Put bedrooms on Airbnb without telling her. Illegal.

9. Valerie. Wally said she had a nice face but was not hot unless she lost a few pounds.

10. Erin's dad. Called Wally a loser. Erin is not allowed to use that word.

I reached over and closed the laptop. This had gone too far. It was up to grown-ups to make kids feel the world made sense. I took a deep breath.

"Listen, Polly, this isn't up to you. I know something terrible happened." Polly's lower lip started to move. Shadow had stopped eating and was listening, too, her eyes large and unblinking. "It's a big help to Duck to have people who care. But this is not your job. The RCMP know what they are doing." I hesitated, unsure if I meant what I was about to say next. "I'm going to think about what I can do. You can help by doing this for the Co-op," I gestured to the piles of receipts, "so I can concentrate on that. Deal?"

Polly looked relieved. "Deal," she said.

Shadow waited, stared into my eyes until I looked away, then went back to her bowl, reassured.

What had just happened? Had I just committed to finding a killer to save Duck? What in my background as a sewing teacher and crafter qualified me to do that?

I had no idea. But I was certain of one thing.

I'd just made a promise.

To a thirteen-year-old girl and a cat.

CHAPTER TEN

The drive home with an enthusiastic golden retriever and a rigid cat was a challenge. Toby sat upright on the back seat, panting with joy, delighted with the idea of going for a car ride with a cat that, up to now, hoped the dog didn't exist. Shadow, on the other hand, spent the trip under my feet, as far away from Toby as she could get, plotting her escape. I was so glad we only had to drive a few blocks to the house.

Once we were home, I was so relieved to have all three of us behind the front door that I dropped the bag of gray pollock in the hall, dumped the box and kitty litter in the closet in the spare room, staggered to the kitchen, leaned on the counter, and filled the kettle for tea.

To my surprise, Toby went into the living room and sat, as still as he could manage, to watch the little gray cat inspect the house, tail high in the air, disdain on her face, and hope for her approval.

It had been a long time since I had lived with a cat, and I'd forgotten how unlike dogs they were. Where would I feed her? I knew I should try to get her to eat again, but I also knew I couldn't put her food on the floor, not with a golden retriever in the house. I filled a saucer with cat food and then, with a silent apology to my mother the impeccable housekeeper, put it down on the counter and a kitchen stool beside it. Cats, I remembered, could go places big dogs could not.

That done, I filled my teacup. As I was emptying the kettle into the sink, I looked out the kitchen window at the blue jay nest and caught my breath. While all the human drama was unfolding down at the store, here at home, wings were sprouting. I grabbed my phone, took a picture, and, on impulse, sent it to Sydney. Maybe Paul would think this was too much from a new boyfriend's mother, but I was too tired to care. If Sydney liked the eggs, she'd love the wings. My son could adjust.

I heard a blue jay squawk, and I looked up. Two birds, the mom and dad, I assumed, were on a nearby tree, alert, as they watched a crow fly past to a power line on the other side of the street.

Crows, predators. What could I do? The chicks had been born nestled against my house. I looked at the parents and felt like an aunt; I was responsible, too. My thumb scrolled over the screen of the phone in my hand, and I found Kenny McQuarrie's number.

Kenny and I had a history. He was the local building inspector and, in the past, had once tried to shut down the Co-op's renovations. I was a local busybody and, in the past, had once accused him of murder. Neither of these events had been the best start to any relationship, but over time we'd reached a truce, and now even walked our dogs together. This was handy because when Kenny wasn't inspecting or dog-walking, he ran the local birding association. If anyone would know what to do about crows and skinny, at-risk baby birds outside my back door, it would be Kenny. I dialed. He picked up on the first ring.

"McQuarrie here."

"Kenny, it's Valerie Rankin. I have a blue jay nest at my house, and they've just hatched. But there are some crows around. What do I do?"

"Crows?" Kenny came alive. "Blue jays? I'm on my way. This requires a site visit. Be there in ten minutes."

I stared at my phone. I had been hoping for some over-the-phone advice, like bang pots or spray with vinegar, not having Kenny come to my house, but then again, I'd called a bird man. This was to be expected.

Kenny was at my front door in seven minutes. The nest fascinated him, but he was wary of Shadow until I assured him that she would remain an indoor cat while she was staying with me.

"Cats and birds don't mix," he said, carefully viewing my backyard, the images of the nest on my phone, and the power line across the street. "However, blue jays are pretty capable. You don't see them, but there will be a whole extended family of jays nearby. Aunts, uncles, cousins. It's a community, just like the one we have around here." He laughed at his own wit. "They'll harass the crows in a mob, if necessary. What you could do if you want is put out some food, peanuts will work, around the front of the house to draw the crows away. That might help."

I nodded. I could do that. "Thanks, that's a good idea. Can I make you some tea?"

"No, I'm fine," Kenny said. "I have Max waiting at home for his walk. But I got to ask. Where did you get this camera set-up for the nest? Pretty slick."

"Duck did it for me," I said, then paused. "You know they've arrested him for Wally's murder, don't you?"

"I heard," Kenny said. "Was there an animal involved?"

"Depends on your view of tourism operators. Why do you say that?"

"He's the reason I have Max. Poor guy was tied up all day outside a place on the Number 2 highway. Duck cut the chain, but he couldn't keep Max himself, so he brought him to me. Said we reminded him of each other." Kenny smiled. Duck was right. Max was a bulldog by breed, Kenny by disposition. "There was a bit of stink from the owner about trespassing. But when I suggested we do an inspection on his septic... funny thing, the guy the dropped the charges."

"Got it," I said. This must be the damage to property Rollie had referred to. "But I don't see Duck doing anything really violent, do you?"

Kenny stood in my kitchen, weighing the odds. Finally, he said, "I don't know what evidence the RCMP has, so maybe there's a case. But I have my own professional experience, you know. All day, every day, I deal with people trying to pull a fast one—no vapor barrier over the insulation, not compacting the soil under a driveway, land not draining away from the house, stairs with the steps different heights...." He shook his head in disbelief at the innate corruption of the human species. "I know Duck's been in jail, but I know rule breakers. I just don't feel that in him." Kenny stopped, considering. "That guy Wally, on the other hand, not to speak badly about the departed, particularly those who've had their throats cut, was the opposite. The man ravaged, absolutely ravaged some piping plover nests. It was inconceivable and unforgivable."

"I heard about that, I'm sorry."

"Thanks." Kenny seemed still shaken by the memory. "There are some who break the rules and some who don't even know there are rules. Wally was one of those."

Kenny stood still, as if deciding not to leave after all. "I think I will have that tea," he said. "There's something else that's been playing on my mind over this whole business."

"Like what?" I asked, pulling a mug out of the cupboard and refilling the kettle.

"The knife, where they found it," he said. "It just seems too obvious."

I sat down to listen. "In what way?"

Kenny looked out the window at the nest again, his back to me. "The word is that the knife that killed Wally was in the pocket of Duck's jacket," he said.

I nodded. "That's what Rollie told me."

"What he said to me, too." Kenny turned around. "But did he tell you it was a *hockey* jacket?"

I tried to remember. "Maybe." As a Canadian, I had seen a thousand hockey jackets in my lifetime, and I struggled to recall what they looked like. "Why is that important?"

Kenny looked impatient. "The name, think of it. Every hockey jacket in this country is the same—the position you play on one arm and your name on the other."

He was right. I could see it now, Duck's old leather jacket on a hook by the back door.

"Look," Kenny said. "How easy would it be for someone trying to get rid of a murder weapon to have come in through the back door of the store, see the jacket with Duck's name on it, and slip the knife into the pocket?"

I leaned back against the padded vinyl of the old chrome kitchen chair. "Are you saying it was a mistake, Duck never had the knife?"

"It's possible," Kenny said. "All I'm saying is it's possible. I even wonder if it was deliberate, if someone was trying to set Duck up." Kenny shook his head and looked at the white enamel paint on the kitchen ceiling. "If there's one thing I've learned after thirty years in the business, it's to never write off to accident or incompetence what can be explained by deception."

I stared at him. "Kenny, you have to tell someone, go to the RCMP."

"Hold on, Valerie, hold on. A theory isn't facts, an idea is not evidence. Not how this works." Kenny stood up. "Just saying something that crossed my mind, that's all. Thing like this stirs you up. Maybe I should stick to birds."

I doubted if that was true. What Kenny said opened my mind up to so many possibilities, so after he left, I sat at my kitchen table for a long time, long after my tea went cold and the room became dusky as the sun outside slipped away. If Kenny had figured this out about the jacket, surely Wade and Nolan had considered it, too.

A movement at the window caught my eye. I walked over and looked out. The mother blue jay had returned to her nest, plumped out her gray belly, and was settling down for the night. Her babies were safe from crows now.

She'd done her job.

CHAPTER ELEVEN

I woke up the next morning to the sound of my reading glasses hitting the floor. I'd been dreaming I was teaching my pocket class in a prison. It took me a moment to focus. I looked around. Toby was still beside me, his body a wall of solid reassurance, his head on the pillow next to mine. Turning my head, I saw Shadow on the bedside table. The cat watched me, confirmed I was awake, and swept my phone onto the floor.

I lay back. The day had not started, and already I was overwhelmed. Darlene said I should begin my mornings by listing five things to be grateful for. Today, all I could think of was one big thing, and it filled me with panic, not gratitude. I was totally in over my head in the killer-finding department. Kenny's idea of a faceless murderer running through our store, ditching weapons in the pocket of a hockey jacket, seemed silly now but had expanded my list of questions—who else could have killed Wally, and why they had wanted to make it look like Duck did it?

Great. Two steps backward and no steps forward.

I was settling in to feel sorry for myself when I heard the buzz of my phone under the bed. I reached down for it.

James Martin. I sat up. 8:04. This was strange.

"Val? I hope this isn't too early," he said, "but something unusual just happened. It's about those earrings for my nieces."

Earrings? We'd sold him six pairs, Colleen's best work, glass beads on gold shepherd's hooks. James was one of our best customers. In addition to the earrings, he was a reliable consumer of mittens, stained glass, and the floor mats the crafters wove out of fishing rope in giant Celtic knots. He told us they made excellent hostess gifts, and he was, I suspected, a man who knew a few hostesses. He'd bought so much the other day, I'd had to help him carry everything out to his car in front of the store.

"The ones we just sold you?" I asked. "Was there a problem?"

"No, no. They were spectacular. But they're gone. I went out this morning to bring everything in, and the car was a mess. Someone had rifled through it, and everything was still there but the earrings. I think they were stolen."

I didn't need to ask if the car had been locked. This was Gasper's Cove.

"Have you looked around?" I asked, diplomatically. James was older than I was, and he was a professor. "Maybe you picked them up yourself and forgot you did it. I do that all the time. Have you checked the house?"

It was as if James had read my mind.

"No, I am quite sure, Valerie. I'm not losing it. They were there last night, and now they are gone. Someone was in the car." Shadow walked across my lap, sniffed Toby, then jumped off the bed.

"Maybe you should call the RCMP?" I suggested, aware from experience how delighted Wade would be to receive a lost-earring call.

"I doubt there's much they could do," James said, probably accurately. "But the girls still have birthdays. Can we replace those earrings? I know it's short notice, but do you have any more?"

Of course we did. Colleen's current craze was jewelry, and until that burned out, I had more earrings than I knew what to do with. Toby got up and walked across my legs to follow the cat. Two animals in the house were going to keep me busy.

"I do, right here in the house. Colleen dropped them off." I had an idea. "Why don't I run them out to you this morning? Free of charge, since you buy local."

James chuckled. "No need to do that, of course, I'll compensate you for your trouble, but that would be lovely. I'll put the coffee on."

I went to the dining room and gathered up Colleen's earrings. She had to show me how to make them myself. I'd tried. Night after night, with beads from Recreate and Recycle color-sorted in an old muffin tin, I'd watched and rewatched YouTube videos, but always my earrings looked like Toby had made them. Eventually, I'd given up and resorted to stringing the beads randomly into necklaces and had even sold some. Maybe I should add "learn how to make earrings so the sharp wire edges don't stick out" to my to-do list, right after "find the real killer." It shouldn't be hard to do both.

On the drive out along the coast to see James, I thought about Polly's list. It seemed obvious that the best way to prove Duck's innocence was to prove someone else's guilt. But who had the motive to kill Wally? A tourist disgusted by $30 spent on detours and false information? That didn't narrow it down. A business competitor threatened by "Un"Authentic Celtic Tours? Unlikely. A jealous husband? Hard to imagine Wally with a love life, but then again, I was one to talk. How about another small business owner? The tour operator had tried to shake me down. Had someone cracked under the pressure of paying kickbacks? I didn't think so. I'd handled Wally the Enforcer by laughing in his face. I hadn't had to kill him, so why would anyone else?

Unable to answer my questions, I thought about James. He was an easy man to talk to and had certainly filled an empty space in Rollie's life. I owed him for that. Rollie had given up a lot to come home, and that made me feel guilty. My cousin had trained to be a psychologist, not the manager of a rural store. I wondered how much he missed private practice and his consultancy at the prison. How could a man of his intellect be satisfied with repetitious conversations about the weather, the roads, and whose hips ached the most in the cold? No wonder he enjoyed the dinner parties out here James threw for his on-sabbatical university friends. Those were more Rollie's kind of people.

The house James rented almost at the end of the Shore Road was remote but spectacular. Building it on the top part of the island facing the open sea, the architect had enough sense to keep the structure simple, angling the front out like the bow of a ship to cut the wind and mounting glass on all sides so not one detail of the view would be missed. A large deck faced the North Atlantic, cantilevered over the cliff, and an old light from a traditional lighthouse was mounted on the deck on a slab of Nova Scotia granite, like a piece of art. Rollie told me a local man came out once a week to trim the property on a riding lawn mower, but otherwise, James took care of the place himself.

The massive glass-paned door to the house was opened before I knocked. James greeted me with a courtesy hug, and I breathed in the long-forgotten smell of a man's aftershave. As usual, the professor looked like he slept, or at least napped, in his clothes, but underneath the crumbs and wrinkles, I could see real quality. In my assessment, his gray trousers were 100% British wool flannel, his blue checkered shirt cotton and wool Viyella, his navy cravat silk, and his maroon cardigan cashmere. I thought I could smell something warming in the oven. Over such fabric, I would have worn an apron.

"Valerie, so kind of you to come out," he said, taking the tissue paper–wrapped earrings I handed him. "Thank you so much for this."

"Don't mention it, I understand. Can't imagine what happened. Maybe kids? Sometimes the parents come here for the view, but the teenagers get bored."

"You're probably right," James agreed, stepping aside. "You haven't been here before, have you?" he asked, waving me into a vestibule that made my unsophisticated mouth drop. The house belonged to a German couple, here only a few months of the year, so I'd expected to see European furniture, but IKEA, this was not. No one had put these leather couches and teak bookshelves together from a kit. I'd never been in a home like this.

James picked up on my reaction. "I thought we could sit in the kitchen and chat if you have the time. It's more comfortable. I appreciate the jewelry; my nieces will be thrilled. Please stay, my croissants and coffee are ready."

"Croissants?" I asked. "Like from scratch?" I had never heard of such a thing. Darlene and I had been in our late teens before we'd even eaten a croissant, bought in a plastic box from the supermarket in Halifax. Baking all those flakes looked tricky to me.

James laughed, a little embarrassed. "I know, I know. One of my many vices. I'm a bit of a do-it-yourselfer, too," he said with a wink. "That's why I admire what you've done with the Co-op."

Flattered, I followed my host into a stainless steel and white kitchen, a universe away from the linoleum-tiled little space in my bungalow. We sat across from each other at a glass-topped table facing the ocean and the sky, bisected only by the horizon. I watched James fold my napkin into a diamond, and I relaxed. I needed this, to be waited on. Now, I was grateful.

"I heard from Darlene you're working on a book about rumrunners," I said, to begin a conversation with my host. "Tell me how a thing like that works."

James was silent for a moment, then smiled. "Standard investigative methodology. Thesis, hypothesis, data analysis, and results. That's it, apart from sending it out for peer review, of course."

Or take it down to the RCMP, I thought. "That's it?" I asked. "Sounds easy."

"It's harder," James said, a knowing look on his face. "All researchers need to be aware of their own biases and make sure they are open to all outcomes. It is always tempting to prove something you want to believe."

Was he talking about me? With someone this smart, it was hard to know.

I decided to change the subject. "What made you interested in rumrunners?" I asked. The coast made smuggling easy, but no one talked about it.

"I think I study outlaws because my own life is so dull," James said, putting down his coffee cup, a wistful look on his kind face. "That's why I come up here. Real people, real lives. You have no idea what mind-numbing boredom is until you've sat through a faculty meeting."

I took his word for it.

"When I started looking into the illegal smuggling of legal goods, which is what the rumrunners did, I found they were ordinary men just trying to evade tax collectors, just helping support their families in a tough environment," he said. "I'm not sure they thought it was a crime, because it was the government they were cheating."

That sounded about right to me. To my grandfather's generation, the ocean gave them enough trouble; they had no time for officials or rules.

"But why weren't they ever caught?" I asked. I couldn't remember any of the old-timers talking about arrests.

"That's the thing, isn't it?" James said. "The communities involved were so closed, no outsider could get in. Customs officials on both sides of the border certainly tried, but unless they could make friends with a local, and they rarely could, they had no chance."

I could only imagine. "And I guess a coast like ours, so rough and with so many hidden coves and inlets, was made for that kind of activity."

"Exactly. Only someone who lived here would ever know what came in. That's been a challenge to my research, too, in fact," he added.

"Really? What do you mean?"

"The primary sources are hard to find. Even if they would talk, most of the men who were involved are gone now. I'm afraid I found that without faces, and real voices, what I wrote was flat. It even bored me; I needed human detail."

He meant people. I understood this. "So, what did you do?" I asked.

"I listened, and I talked," he said, the skin around his mouth creasing as he smiled. "You know how I like to do that. I let folks in the community know what I was working on and made myself accessible. So often, people don't know what they have. Information comes to who is nearest when someone is ready to communicate. The trick is to be that person."

"And did someone want to talk?" I asked.

"In a manner of speaking, yes," James answered. "One of the long-time residents here, I can't say who, was going through their possessions, and guess what they found?"

"No idea, tell me." Was James talking about Colleen? This sounded like something that might have happened in one of her forced cleaning-out crusades. What had she found, apart from two hundred unfinished craft projects?

James leaned forward, serious now. "A diary. Written by a man who knew them all. It tells the story of a young man who signed on with a boat at fifteen. Can you imagine?"

"Unfortunately, I can," I said. Life started early in those days along a working coast.

James continued, animated by his life's work. "They sent him just outside the twelve-mile limit in New York Harbor. In a dinghy, at night, to meet the gangsters who bought the booze. A kid, with half a ten-dollar bill in his hand. Anyone who came alongside with the other half, he led them back to the ship, and they'd load up." James's eyes were bright with excitement.

"Sounds incredibly dangerous to me," I said. Where was this kid's mother?

James looked at me, surprised. "Of course, it was dangerous, that's the point. And I suspect many of these men went on to live quiet lives, never talked about the past."

Suddenly, I thought about Duck and the note. He was a quiet man. Someone knew something about Duck I didn't. What had happened in his past? I felt uncomfortable and restless.

"I've used up enough of your time, James. I have a dog to walk." I stood up. "I hope your nieces enjoy the jewelry. Thank you for supporting us," I added, as we walked down the hall to the entry.

James waved my thanks aside to pull the wide door open, then stopped.

"The manuscript is off with my editor now," he said. "My book. Do you know how I ended it?"

I had no idea.

"With the last line in the rumrunner's dairy: 'This is a true record of the best years of my life.' Who could top that?"

He had a point. No one could.

But then again, how many of us know what has happened in someone else's best years, or the worst ones?

CHAPTER TWELVE

I had just opened the car door for the drive home when my phone beeped. It was a text from Annette, my sewing student, the manager of Recreate and Recycle, and my Tupperware lady.

Got your order.

Great!

I texted back.

When can I pick it up?

How about now? At the church hall for the fundraiser. They have sandwiches.

Annette knew me well. There was no way I could resist church-basement, made-by-the-women's auxiliary sandwiches, not even with a stomach already full of croissants and coffee.

On my way.

The Gasper's Cove United Church was spare and utilitarian upstairs, as the denomination required, but usually a hotbed of activity in the hall below. During the week, a variety of groups met there: Moms 'n Tots, the Quilting Guild, AA, Chair Yoga for seniors, Teen Meetup, and the Historical Society (three members, the husbands of the Chair Yoga athletes). All of this was in addition to the times reserved for every branch of the Baden Powell scouting empire, founded when there was an empire.

But despite all this community engagement, the church hall shone most when it reverted to its roots. Socials, luncheons, bridal teas, and post-funeral receptions were when the hall came into its own. For events like these, the tea and coffee urns came out, a legion of elderly ladies from the congregation took over the kitchen, the stacking chairs were unstacked, long polyester tablecloths were snapped over the plywood tables, and the trays of fancy sandwiches and baking were laid out.

Today, the ladies were catering a fundraiser for the Drummond Hospital. Right at the door, I was encouraged to buy tickets for the 50/50 raffle (half of the proceeds to go to the hospital and half to the winner). As I stood and waited for the parishioner to fill out the entry form for me, I saw Annette across the hall, her Tupperware fanned out on a table, and her door prize, a seventeen-piece serving set, prominently displayed.

"I like the look of that," I said when I reached her. "Sign me up for the drawing."

"Will do," Annette said, laughing, unwinding my tickets from a large roll of tiny numbered purple paper squares, one for me and one for a huge glass jar. "I've got your order here, too."

"I don't know how you do it," I said, waving my arm over her table. "Managing the Depot and all this, on tour all over the area delivering orders."

Annette laughed. "Runs in the family. Mom did Avon, and I do Tupperware. Dad was a plumber, and Mom was a housewife but, like she said, every little bit counts." She reached underneath the draped table and pulled out a large plastic bag of bowls. "Besides, I love it. Look at these. The vintage pastels, you lucky girl." She leaned forward. "Listen, if you want a laugh, check out the kitchen. That influencer is in there, trying to pump the ladies for recipes. She's met her match and doesn't even know it."

Jennifer Fox was here? I picked up my bowls; I loved new Tupperware. "I'll do that," I said, "but not before I get a plate."

"Smart move," Annette said, "I recommend the butter tarts. Colleen made them. Get moving, they won't last."

Taking her advice, I made my way to the tables in the center of the room. On the first table were the fancy sandwiches, all without crusts, some sliced into ribbons, others rolled into pinwheels or cut into white-and-brown checkerboards, and then filled with egg, salmon, tuna, cream cheese with cherries, or ham diced with pickles. On the next table, I saw the sweets— gingersnaps, Nanaimo bars, date and lemon squares, and Colleen's butter tarts next to a draped card table that held the urns of coffee and tea, the sugar cubes, and milk, canned and fresh. I smiled when I saw the two pitchers. In this area, many of the older people had been raised with canned milk in the winter and, as a result, would have been disappointed if it hadn't been here for their tea.

Balancing my heavy plate, the bag of plastic bowls, and my teacup, I poked my head into the kitchen. Inside, I saw a legion of ladies, aprons tied high above full midriffs, bustling as only United Church women could. Trailing around behind them, a notebook in her hand, her thick, streaked blond hair pushed back with a velvet headband, an odd contrast to the tight white and gray perms bobbing around her, was Jennifer Fox.

"Let me read this back to you, see if I've missed anything," she said, her face puzzled and alert. "*Unbelievable pastry.* One cup butter, two cups flour, a tablespoon of salt, and a dash of vinegar, is that right?"

"Sounds about right," one matron responded, "not that I measure. But with pastry, it's all in the technique. Did you write that part down, just what I told you?"

Jennifer studied her notes. "Yes. 'Knead hard for fifteen to twenty minutes, until sticky, then spoon into a pie plate.' Is that right? No rolling pin?"

"Rolling pins went out with gaslight. This is how we do it now. Try that in your restaurant, but don't tell anyone where you got it. It's a secret."

Jennifer made an exaggerated zipping motion with her fingers across her mouth. "Only my followers will have this," she said, "and they trust me."

"I'm sure they do," Mrs. Smith, Noah's landlady who lived across and down the street from me said, tucking in her lips to control a smile. "And we haven't even told you about the secret to mile high biscuits—bake at five hundred degrees for forty minutes."

"Ah, I knew there was a trick," the famous influencer said, conspiratorially snapping her ballpoint pen into action about her notebook. "This is like gold."

I saw Colleen by the stove, and I pulled her out into the hall.

"What's going on in there?" I asked.

"The ladies figured that one out," she whispered. "She's been following us around, talking so much we could hardly get anything done, so the girls decided it wouldn't hurt to tease her a bit. Some of the ladies are over ninety, and they haven't enjoyed themselves this much in years."

I could only imagine. "Listen, I hear you made a friend in James Martin," I said. "Nice of you to give him the diary. Did it belong to your dad?"

Colleen pulled her head back and looked at me. "Diary? What are you talking about? From my dad? That man could hardly write his own name. James came by, and I gave him tea and told him a few stories, but that was it. You must have gotten that wrong."

This didn't make any sense. Who else would have been the source of a rumrunner's memoir? I wanted to ask Colleen more, but before I could, Jennifer hurried out of the kitchen, her face down toward her phone as she pushed past me, moving quickly toward the bright red exit sign at the end of the hall.

On impulse, I decided to follow her. Jennifer Fox was not who she said she was, and I wanted to know why. I put my plate down on a draped table. With a quick apology to Colleen, I hurried away, clutching my big bag of plastic bowls. I kept to the edges of the hall until I was at the exit myself and waited until I heard Jennifer close the big door upstairs behind her. Then, I made my way up the stairs and out into the parking lot behind the church.

The afternoon was overcast outside, but the sound of gravel under high-heeled boots helped me spot Jennifer as she cut across past the parked cars to the alley that led out to Front Street. Holding my Tupperware in front of me like a shield, I followed, working my way to the back of the parking lot, dodging truck to truck, car to car, as quietly as I could. Ahead of me, I heard a car door slam. I stepped behind a panel van with *Boudreau Fisheries* painted on the side and carefully looked down the alley. Putting my spread fingers in front of my face, like a kid watching a horror movie, and fooling no one, I moved out from my hiding place to get a better look.

Jennifer had vanished.

Instead, I saw two cars, engines running, side by side, one nose in and one nose out. I saw a figure inside one of the vehicles move, leaning toward the window, as if to talk to the driver of the other car, and when he did, I saw the lapels of an ill-fitting jacket riding up over bulky shoulders.

The second car was dark and sleek, and in it, I could only make out the profile of the driver. Her ponytail swung as she leaned into the open window, so I could see the passenger next to her as she pushed a wide headband back.

I recognized them both—Stuart's friend Kimberly and Jennifer.

How did those two know each other? And who were they talking to?

Something was cooking, and it wasn't mile high biscuits.

CHAPTER THIRTEEN

The next morning, Toby and I made our way down to the store, leaving Shadow behind to explore in peace. I felt discouraged. My digging around to prove that Duck was as innocent as Shadow and I believed was going nowhere. I was terrible at this.

Darlene, however, would be pleased with me. Today, I had two things for which I was truly grateful. First, one of my children was in the vicinity, however temporarily, and second, I had sewing classes to think about. As soon as Toby and I got to the store, I would get ready for this evening's workshop and then prepare for pants fitting next week. Tonight, with my students, if nowhere else, I would be in the company of people who were committed, sensible, and transparent. There would be no lies and no mysteries in my classroom, and if a student had a crotch fitting issue, I could fix it. It was only a tiny part of the world, but in my sewing classroom, life made sense. All I needed was to get there and hide from the world.

That wasn't going to happen. As soon as I had deposited Toby in his greeter's recliner at the front of the store, Polly and Rollie intercepted me.

"You have a visitor," Rollie said. "In the classroom. Stuart. He has something to show you."

"Right," said Polly. "You're about to learn about Operation Fish. I went through it when Erin and I did a school project."

"Fish?" I was puzzled, something familiar about this, but I couldn't place it. "What are you talking about?"

"I won't ruin the surprise," Polly said, looking sideways at Rollie, who was trying not to smile. "It's an experience no one can describe."

Mystified, I went down to my classroom and opened the door.

Stuart had taken over the long table we used for cutting and covered it with papers and old photocopies. I saw he had also drawn a diagram on my classroom blackboard, something geographical—I recognized the two boot shapes, one to the extreme left of the board and one to the right: Nova Scotia and the United Kingdom, with the Atlantic Ocean between.

What was going on?

Looking up when I arrived, Stuart rushed over to pull out a chair for me. I sat. Clearly, I was here for a lesson of some kind.

I'd never seen Stuart's handsome face so earnest. The sleeves of his dress shirt were rolled halfway up his forearms, and the top two buttons of his shirt were undone. The edge of a white cotton undershirt showed near his neck, and instinctively I checked for the telltale shadows of short sleeves under his shirt and saw them. It had been years since

I'd seen a man who still wore undershirts like that, and it brought me back to my dad. Was Stuart one of the men they didn't make anymore?

"Wow, you've done a lot of work here," I said, bringing myself back to the room. Then, even though I knew better, like a mean girl, I blurted, "Where's Kimberly?"

Stuart looked stunned. For a moment, it seemed as if he didn't know whom I was talking about.

"Oh, at Pilates, I think. We were supposed to do Thai massage, but I bailed." I thought I saw a slight shudder before he gathered himself. "I promised I'd come and talk to you about that parachute you found. It was like a light bulb went on when you told me—Fairyfox. It connected." He reached behind him to pull out a chair and sat down across from me, eager to start the conversation.

"Fairyfox?" I asked. "Are you talking about the name on the bottom of the parachute?"

Instead of answering me, Stuart just stared and said, "What do you know about Winston Churchill?"

I looked up at the pressed-metal ceiling above me and blew out a breath. Of all the names he could have said this morning, this was not one I was expecting.

"'We will fight on the beaches?'" I searched for the rest. "'We shall fight in the fields and in the streets.... We shall never give up?'"

"That's more or less it, at least the lines most people know," Stuart said, shrugging. "But those are not lines that, in my view, show who Churchill really was."

"Not following," I said, accurately.

Stuart sat back in his chair, relaxed and happy. I was witnessing a man sharing a passion. He leaned forward again, solemnly, so our knees almost touched.

"'Truth,' Churchill said, 'is so precious that she should always be surrounded by a bodyguard of lies.'" He sat back, triumphant. "Good book of that title by the way, Anthony Cave Brown. Anyway, that's your parachute, part of the bodyguard."

I sat still for a moment, torn. On the one hand, I was enjoying this man's full attention, and as a person of many enthusiasms myself, I was both flattered and interested to have a window into what got Stuart Campbell, quiet and steadfast civil engineer, so excited. On the other hand, I had no idea at all what he was talking about.

None.

This wasn't a war room in 1939 London we were in, it was this year, and we were in my sewing classroom, in Rankin's General Store, in Gasper's Cove, Nova Scotia.

But I didn't want to see this enthusiasm fade. I had to be delicate.

"I'm not clear here," I started. "What's the connection between an old silk parachute that turned up in the Drummond Recreate and Recycle Depot and Winston Churchill?"

The spell was broken. Stuart returned to reality and his usual reserve.

"Ah, sorry, you need a bit of history. My history. For some weird reason, I always think you know everything about me," he said.

And don't I wish that were true, I thought. "Tell me now."

"Okay, I was a Navy brat. My dad was an officer in the Canadian Navy. He was away a lot, and we moved back and forth between the two coasts when I was growing up." He seemed uncomfortable, as if he were trying to tell me more than words, then continued. "It was only when Dad retired that we got close. We found a common interest, Canadian Naval history. He even started to write books about it, and this"—he gestured to the translucent pages he had laid out on my cutting table—"is his last one, unpublished, *The Secret of Operation Fish.*

Somewhere, in the back of my mind, back as far as my dad and his friends, the title stirred the trace of a memory now, but that was all.

"It was about fishing?" I asked, tentatively, stating the obvious again.

Stuart laughed, "No, not at all. Operation Fish was an incredibly dangerous, top-secret mission the British launched at the beginning of the war, based entirely on deception. You see, right when Churchill was giving his blood-and-guts speeches in the House of Commons, all about not giving up and everything, in secret, he was preparing for invasion, and defeat."

"What?!" I couldn't believe it. This was like hearing there was no Santa Claus.

"Yes, it's true. Churchill was no fool. He could see how Hitler was rolling over all of Europe, and he was afraid the British Isles would be next. So, he did something really, really crazy." Stuart the passionate enthusiast was back, and I was enjoying it. "He gathered all the wealth of the nation, he called in private assets, made people surrender securities that could be traded outside the country, gathered all the

100

gold bars in the British treasury, everything from the Bank of England, the Crown Jewels, and sent it out of the country so Hitler, if he arrived, couldn't have it."

"You have got to be kidding. Everything? All the wealth of the nation?" This sounded like such a crazy story. "Wouldn't that be like emptying Fort Knox and sending it away? How did he do it?'

"With a bodyguard of lies. Operation Fish. Three ships to be exact. The first one was the HMS *Emerald* in 1939. And you know where she sailed?"

I shook my head, trying to take this all in.

"Here, to Nova Scotia, to the port of Halifax, where it was loaded on trains and taken to Montreal and stored in the vault in the basement of the Sun Life Building."

Sun Life? They did my insurance.

"Why Montreal?" I asked.

"Maybe proximity, the Americans," Stuart explained. "Roosevelt was in on it, even though at that point, the United States hadn't joined the war. He accepted it as security for the arms he funneled to Britain, the Lend-Lease Program they called it, all run through Canada. It helped win the war."

I sat back. I looked at all the pages Stuart's father had typed and thought of how they had been used to talk to a son. I looked at the map Stuart had drawn on the blackboard. It made sense now.

"Sounds incredibly risky," I said. "Hard to imagine the Germans not figuring this out. There must have been spies who saw this happen."

"That," Stuart said, taping a forefinger down on my leg, "is the bodyguard again. The crew never knew. They dressed them in tropical whites when they were in harbor in England, so they all thought they were going south. It was only after they sailed that they knew they were headed to Canada."

"Trick dressing, pretty clever, someone was smart." I sat back, trying to absorb this story, then thought of something. "Hang on. I'm missing a piece here, a very big piece. What does any of this have to do with an old parachute?"

"Weather," Stuart said. "Bad North Atlantic weather. The *Emerald* was hit by a storm before she got to this coast. The cargo was safe, but they lost a lot of what was on deck." He paused for dramatic effect. "This included a small spotter seaplane, a tiny thing, one they used to send up into the air with a catapult, if you can believe it. The plane on the *Emerald* was washed overboard. And you know what her name was?"

I looked right into Stuart's earnest, clear blue eyes and thought I saw the sea there. "The *Fairyfox*?" I asked, knowing I was right.

"You got it," he said. "Now, the question is not only how did it get here but who found it, and why was it hidden so long?"

CHAPTER FOURTEEN

I stared at Stuart. Deep in the junk drawer of my mind, two thoughts were struggling to find each other. What he had said was somehow connected to something else. I didn't know what. Maybe if I let it percolate, the connection would come to me later.

"What are you saying?" I asked, still trying to make sense of everything Stuart had told me.

"Think of it," he said, eyes bright. "The *Fairyfox* was a seaplane. It had floats instead of wheels. We know the *Emerald* was hit by a storm not far from this coast, and the *Fairyfox* was washed overboard. Maybe, and I know this sounds crazy, and if it wasn't for your parachute, I wouldn't even speculate. But maybe it somehow ended up here, wrecked along our coast." A cloud passed over his face. "Man, I wish my dad was here. He would have loved this."

I started to count back the decades in my head. "But Stuart, that was nearly ninety years ago. With our weather, the rocks, the ocean, there wouldn't be anything left, or," remembering what James said about the old rumrunners, I added, "anyone still alive who might have seen it."

"Then tell me where the parachute came from," Stuart asked. "You were there. Who brought it in? Can you find that out?"

Annette. She ran the Depot, and if anyone might know where the bag containing the parachute came from, she would. And she'd be in the class I'd be teaching soon. I'd ask her.

"I know who to talk to. I'll do my best," I told him. "I'll let you know what I find out."

Stuart smiled at me, and it lit up the room. "Would you do that? I'd really appreciate it. I'd love to get to the bottom of this. This is such a part of my personal history, a story I heard my whole life, and to have it reappear now...." He stopped to search for the right word. "It just feels incredible, so surreal."

"Don't worry, we'll get this figured out," I said, thinking this would give us something in common, a reason to keep in touch. "I'm just as interested in this as you are. Ever since I saw that parachute, I felt she had a story to tell. But my students will be here soon for my class...." The truth was, kicking Stuart out of my classroom right now was the last thing I wanted to do. What if he ended up at that Thai massage?

"Oh, right, sorry," Stuart gathered his papers. "I promised to drop this stuff off at the library for Catherine anyway. Some researcher might be interested in this someday, and I have a copy at home." He stopped and looked at me. "Thanks for listening to me. I know I get carried away with this stuff. There aren't many women like you."

I felt a lift in my chest. "Oh, really? Why's that?" I asked, getting ready for a compliment, a breakthrough.

"You know, interested in Naval history," he said. "Most women have better things to do."

The lift went flat.

I tried to regroup. "I have many interests," I said, letting it hang, thinking to myself, what would those be? Sewing, crafts, dog walking, and nostalgia? Not exactly a riveting list.

Stuart smiled again, oblivious to anything but Winston Churchill and spotter planes, and left, leaving me to fill the big tank of my gravity-fed iron and to turn my mind to sewing, the only area of my life where, right now, I felt I still had a place.

I was looking forward to tonight's session. It was a special workshop on one of my favorite subjects—pockets— something I had slotted in before we started our pants-fitting marathon. As a woman who found purses, handbags, pocketbooks, whatever you wanted to call them just one more thing to remember, haul around, or leave behind, I definitely was a pocket person.

I'd done a lot of prep for tonight's class. I had laid out samples of various options, with written instructions for each one: patch, slant, zippered, welt (single and double), double-entry pockets (a lined patch with a flap, but with the stitching left open at the side so you could also put your hands behind them on cold days), and my favorite—the "hidden double-entry." I put these last pockets in all my reversible jackets and coats. The way I did them made only one pocket bag rather than two, which would be too bulky, to be accessed by each side of the coat. In jackets, on the one plain "tasteful" side, I put in a single welt pocket, and on the "jazzy," usually patterned, fabric other side, I put in a zippered pocket, but both were able to access the same tear-drop pocket installed between the layers of the two shells. This technique also let the wearer reach in from, say, the zippered pocket on the outside of the garment, put her hand through the welt opening of the second layer, and pull out something out from the pocket of the garment underneath. I'd found this handy on many mornings of dog walking in the rain, when I'd wanted to retrieve my phone from the pocket of my jeans but didn't want to unzip my entire jacket to do it. Personally, I thought double-entry pockets were brilliant inventions, and usually one student in every term thought so, too.

This evening, my group would include the usual suspects: new mothers, retirees eager for a night out of the house, and the serious sewists who were humoring me until I could look at the diagonal wrinkles in their tried-it-at-home pants muslins. Annette arrived a little late and had brought Colleen as a favor to Darlene, who was still campaigning to have her mother develop more connections in town.

After they'd all settled in around the big U-shaped table I used for demos, we went over the pocket types. I showed my students tips for the tricky parts, like how to make a pocket bag with one scrap of fabric, no pattern, and how to use graph paper to keep the stitching lines straight on the welts.

At break time, I found Colleen and Annette talking in the corner of the room.

"What do you mean, your daughter is trying to kill you?" I heard Annette ask Colleen.

"She's rushing me, trying to empty my house. I'm just not ready." Colleen was adamant. I could see what Darlene was up against. "She just doesn't understand."

"Doesn't understand what?" I asked, joining the conversation.

"She doesn't understand that it's not about the things, it's about who I was in that house that I'm not ready to leave behind."

"I can see that," Annette said. "You moved there when you got married, didn't you? Raised your whole family there."

Colleen looked relieved that someone finally understood.

"I know it was chaos. I know Rory wasn't the most reliable of husbands. I know that better than anyone." She paused, a small smile on her face. "But that man could make you laugh. You can always forgive but never forget someone who made you laugh like that. I can still hear his voice, cutting it up in those rooms."

She was lucky to have those memories. "I know," I said. "I've heard the stories from my parents." The stories had included the one when life-of-the-party Rory had been felled by a heart attack, down in the rec room, rum and coke in hand, at the end of one of his tales, but mercifully after he had delivered the punch line. "Just how he would have wanted to go," my dad said. "With an audience."

Colleen's face softened as she remembered the legend she had lost, and then she continued. "It was me who ran that ship," she said. "They all counted on me, Rory and the kids, and I did it. I knew how to take care of everyone who lived in that house. That's what I don't want to give up, being that person."

Something cracked in me. I didn't know what to say.

Annette did. "Colleen, you're still that same someone who can, and always will be able to, take care of people and make something out of nothing. Look at your crafts."

I had something to add. "Yes, Annette's right. You know those beautiful earrings you made?" Colleen nodded; I had her attention. "James Martin bought twelve pairs. Twelve pairs to send to the States as gifts." There was no need to tell her that six of those pairs had been stolen from the backseat of his car. "Anything you can make, I can sell at the Co-op. You're our star."

Colleen looked thoughtful. "I sure could use the money. Darlene's got me going into the senior housing apartments, and that helps, but the government checks only go so far."

Annette saw an opening and took it. "Listen, the Depot is getting really busy. I need more inventory. Let's make a deal."

"What kind of deal?"

"I know how hard it is to clear out. Why don't you give me whatever you don't need any more, and I'll give you a store credit so you can stock up with the supplies you need for yourself." Bless you, Annette, I thought. I'm going to order more bowls, maybe that butter dish, too.

Colleen looked skeptical. "But you might think what I have is junk—it's mainly craft leftovers that have been laying around for years."

"Nothing is junk to my customers, believe me," Annette said. "Look at those beads I sent home with Darlene for you. They came from our place."

"Twelve pairs?" Colleen asked, looking at me.

"Absolutely. James loved them."

"So, get me more of them, those beads," Colleen said to Annette. "We have a deal."

Coffee break and the deal of the century done, my class resumed. I'd set up my classroom machine, and a few of the students worked on some samples while others traced the patterns I had brought in to share.

At the end of the session, I followed Annette out to her truck.

"That was nice, what you did for Colleen in there," I told her. "It's hard for someone her age to start a new life."

"Hard for anyone at any age," Annette said. "It was Tupperware and Recreate and Recycle that turned it around for me when Darrell took off and left us for that receptionist in Alberta." She reached for the car door, ready to get in and drive home.

"Wait," I said. "About that. Something I have to ask you. You know that old parachute we came across the other day?"

"How could I forget? Talk of the Depot. Catherine's got it now, doing some kind of research, if you want to see it."

"Yes, I know. But I'm wondering. Such a strange thing. Do you have any idea where it came from? You were going to ask the volunteer who takes in donations?"

Annette put her tote bag on the ground. "Right, I did ask her, let me think. What did she say?"

I waited, impatient. I was sure that whatever Annette could tell me would be a key to understanding so many things I didn't understand.

"Drop cloths," Annette said, looking pleased with herself. "Our volunteer was almost certain it came in a big garbage

109

bag someone gave her and said it was full of old drop cloths. You know, for painting? Sheets, things like that."

"Did she remember who gave her the bag?" I asked. Wait 'til I told Stuart. This was exciting.

"She did." Annette was definite. "Someone we're all talking about right now."

"Who? Who?"

"Duck MacDonald. He's the guy who brought that bag in."

CHAPTER FIFTEEN

After Annette drove off, I went back into the store and walked to Rollie's office. I wondered if he was taking Polly's advice and working late getting things in order, ready to file our taxes.

I should have known better. Rollie wasn't at his desk but instead in front of the ancient desktop computer in the corner, a map of the coast of Nova Scotia on the screen.

When I came up behind him, Rollie closed the screen and swung around to face me.

I pulled over the visitor's chair, removed the brown acrylic knit cardigan someone had draped over the back, put it on a hook on the wall, and sat down.

"We have to talk," I said. "Now."

I'd formed a careful and calm statement of my concerns as I'd walked through the store, but now that I was alone with Rollie, I let my emotions take over.

"Something's not right here, and you're in the middle of it, or at least near the middle of it," I said. "You're hiding something, and I want to know what."

"I don't know what you are talking about. Why do you think you have those feelings?" Rollie asked, composing his face into his therapist's objective and bounce-it-back-to-you look, which he knew annoyed me.

"No tricky stuff," I said. "Don't forget, I'm the one who knew you ate all the Christmas baking and blamed it on me. I know when you're up to something."

"Take it easy," Rollie said. He knew I hated that expression even more than I hated his psychologist's face. "Let's start again. What are you talking about?"

"Duck."

"Duck?"

"Yes. You aren't acting normal about any of this, Rollie. I'm mad at you," I added unnecessarily, suddenly aware that these were the exact words I'd yelled at him when I found the shortbread under his pillow four decades ago.

"Not normal?" Rollie drew his head back and pretended to be amazed, as if he were the world's most normal person and I was not. "In what way?"

"Wally, poor old, sleazy, always lost Waldo, never a tipper, small-time Wally. He was killed here behind our store, and our very own handyman—whom you went to a huge amount of trouble to rescue and find a job for when he got out of prison—is arrested. And you're like, 'Oh well, too bad, let the RCMP handle it.' What kind of attitude is that? You should be helping me prove that Duck didn't do it!"

I sat back and waited for Rollie's face to go red like it always did when he was indignant. Instead, he looked at me calmly and carefully.

"Get a hold of yourself." Rollie's voice had a tone I didn't like at all. "Pull yourself together. The only reasonable option here is to let the RCMP, and the justice system they represent, enact the due process."

I didn't like my cousin's formal language. This wasn't what I was talking about at all. And he knew it.

"I'm not an idiot," I said. Rollie had three degrees to my none, and I hoped he didn't think that made a difference. "You're not acting one bit upset about Duck's arrest. Where are your feelings? You're not a cold-hearted person. You cry at commercials. I've seen you. What's going on?" I felt like I was talking to a stranger.

Something I'd said had gotten through. Rollie's face worked up to pink. Now, I thought, we'll get somewhere.

"Listen, Valerie, I don't know what you think you know, but it's nothing. Step back and stay out of it, for your own sake, for Duck's sake, for all our sakes." He was shaking now. I'd pushed him over some invisible line. "This is none of your business. Is that clear?"

Is that clear? Who did Rollie think he was, my dad?

I wasn't done, not by a long shot.

"And another thing, a big thing," I said. "I just talked to Annette, and she said that the old parachute, the one that turned up at the Depot? Duck brought it in." I wanted answers. "Where would he get a thing like that?"

For a moment, Rollie looked confused, and then his face relaxed and went less florid, as if we'd just backed away from something dangerous.

"Absolutely no idea," Rollie said, regaining his composure. "Maybe he was cleaning and took something in. No idea. Forget about it."

Fat chance, I thought, as I got up and walked to the door. I turned to look at my cousin, but his back was to me, once more at the computer. I gestured to the hooks on the wall.

"And by the way, you might want to tell someone she left her sweater here. It's getting colder, she might need it."

After I left the office, I went and got Toby. He, at least, had a good workday, wagging his tail every time someone came in or left the store, ambling around the back parking lot when he needed to—his life predictable and secure. I envied him as I clipped on his leash for the walk home, then looked at the sky. The light was fading, and I could see the storm clouds blowing in. I knew we'd have to hurry to get home before the rain. So, off we went, my dog happy to jog along beside me as I stomped up the hill as fast as I could so I could get to the house and start brooding. What had happened in there with Rollie? I had no idea. Nothing in my life was working out the way it was supposed to.

That thought made me think of Stuart and his accountant-auditor friend. I was sure they were very happy—counting, filing, heads together on a Friday night, giggling over an Excel spreadsheet, calculating the tip to be left on the bill at the Agapi. I bet that woman didn't know how to make anything, except, perhaps, sense and the kind of ordered world a consulting engineer would want. And me? Who was I except a woman who had nothing better to do than be interested in Naval history? But the thing was, I really *was* interested.

My phone beeped, and I pulled it out of my pocket.

It was a message from Sydney.

Hey. love the baby bird pics you sent Keep em coming.

Will do. Surfing good?

There was more.

See U soon. Breakfast sail with George tomorrow.

What? Why were they seeing George?

Sounds fun.

See me soon? When?

We were almost home when the rain started. I had dinner to make and my animals to feed and gather for bedtime. At least they still needed me.

⌒⧓⌒

The boom woke me.

I'd slept in, after wasting too many hours awake in the night, feeling sorry for myself. The noise jolted me awake like a heart attack, sending my pulse racing and my body onto high alert, but with no idea why. When my mind cleared, my first thought was fireworks. But why? First thing in the morning? Canada Day was months away.

Next to me, Toby was tense, his head lifted, listening. Suddenly, he heard something I couldn't, stood up on the bed, barked, and then ran off in the direction of the living room.

What was going on?

I grabbed my robe from the end of the bed and followed him down the hall. Shadow was already at the front window, looking out, impassive, as she slowly licked her paw and dragged it across her face. Beside her, on the couch now, Toby continued to bark, clearly agitated by the sound, the loud boom, whatever it was.

He wasn't the only one. As I watched, the doors of my neighbors' houses opened, and people hustled into the middle of the street, looking back at the hills. Black smoke was rising in the sky, drifting toward us.

I felt myself panic. Moving as fast as I could, I put on my shoes and ran out to join them.

"What was that noise?" I shouted as I ran to Mrs. Smith from across the street. My neighbor's white hair was vertical above her glasses, and her floral fleece robe was pulled tight around her, mauve fluffy slippers still on her feet.

"We don't know," she answered, pointing to another neighbor on his cell phone. "Andy's got a brother who lives on the other side. He's making a call."

The black cloud was above us now. I looked around the gathering group of people from the street and called out, "Anyone know what happened? Where it came from?"

"A summer home?"

"They're away."

"Construction? Are they blasting rock?"

"Nothing being built around here."

"A car? An accident?"

"Don't even say that."

The barking from my house grew louder. Toby was at the window watching me, worried.

Stepping a little away from the crowd to hear better, Andy listened and then put his phone into the breast pocket of his plaid jacket with a sigh. He walked toward us slowly, the legs of his pajama pants tucked into his work boots. The laces were undone and clicked along the asphalt as he walked.

"It's a boat," he said. "It was moored out at the yacht club. It's exploded."

My body felt rigid, and my legs started to shake. I didn't want to ask, but I knew I had to.

"Which boat?" I asked. "Did your brother know? Which boat?"

"He did," Andy said, shaking his head. "It's the one George sails—you know, the guy from the restaurant, the younger one? George Kosoulos."

CHAPTER SIXTEEN

Right there on the street in front of my house, the whole world went black, narrowing into a tiny aperture of light, everything around it gone. I felt the wind blow as if it took me away, and all I was left with was one thought.

My kid. Paul.

I saw the text from Sydney in my mind, sent last night. She'd said they were meeting George for breakfast and a sail. The boat that had blown up—they were on it.

I ran back to my house, to my driveway, to my car, and while I moved, as if it were a reflex, I texted Darlene.

> The explosion. At the yacht club.
> Paul's there on the boat.

I ran back to house and grabbed my keys. Outside again, I dropped them on the ground, twice, then opened the car door, got in, and threw my phone onto the passenger seat. I backed out into the street, trusting anyone behind me to move out of the way, and drove down the hill, right through all the stop signs. At the bottom, on Front Street, I turned to the right, not bothering to signal, and drove past the fish plant and around to the top of the island to the yacht club. I felt like I was in a dream, a horrible, horrible dream.

Off in the distance, I heard sirens.

This couldn't be happening.

Ahead, at the entrance into the club, I saw a crowd was already gathered, cars parked haphazardly, like they had been shaken out of a bag in the sky. I saw Harry Sutherland, the seasonal manager of the club, bent over on the road, placing orange cones across the driveway into the parking lot, moving them only to direct traffic as it arrived—the firetruck, two RCMP cruisers, and an ambulance.

Skidding on the gravel road, I pulled over to the side, across from Harry, almost driving into the ditch. I left the car running, jammed it into park, threw open the door, and got out. I could smell burning, and now that I was closer, I could see the tail of the black smoke as it rose into the morning sky like a tornado.

I charged at Harry. "Let me by, let me in!" I shrieked. "My son's in there."

Harry looked up, saw the look on my face, and hesitated, as if not sure if he should confront me or run back into the clubhouse and hide.

"Valerie, stop!" Harry turned to the voice behind him, with relief. I hadn't seen Officer Wade Corkum arrive, but here he was. He walked toward me, his arms extended like a human plow, moving Harry aside. "Let them work. Stay where you are, Valerie. No one can go in there, not yet."

"I don't care. You don't understand," I screamed, pushing hard at the concrete of Wade's bulletproof vest. "My son is in there!" Wade wrapped his arms around me and turned me around, so I faced away from the water.

I heard a car door down the road.

"Darlene!" Wade called out, as my cousin climbed out of her little white car. "I need a hand here."

Darlene ran over, and Wade passed me to her. I collapsed into her arms, words coming out, none of them in sentences.

"What are you saying, Val?" Darlene pleaded, making eye contact with Wade, with questions on her face. "Slow down, I can't understand you. You're not making any sense." She spoke softly but held me tight, half restraint, half hug.

"Sydney texted me last night and said they were going to go out on the boat with George this morning. On that boat," I shouted, trying to break free from her, pointing to the water beyond the boathouse.

"Oh, my dear," Darlene pulled my head hard down onto her shoulder. "Wade, Wade, Valerie says her son is in there with George, and a girl, too?" She looked at me. I nodded.

"I'll let them know," Wade said. "Try not to worry," he added, which seemed to me to be the stupidest thing he could have said. "Just stay back. Best thing you can do."

With Darlene's arms locked around me, both of us in tears now, we joined the group behind us to watch and wait as Wade strode back to work, leaving a nervous and apprehensive Harry to handle the crowd.

It seemed to me like we stood there forever, but eventually, the cloud of smoke cleared, and the day went quiet. The sea moved in and pulled the floating debris on the surface of the water down into itself and away. Then, we moved aside to let the fire truck leave and then the ambulance and watched them go.

I felt a hand on my shoulder. Wade was back. I was afraid to turn and look at him. But when I did, he leaned in closer and smiled.

"Someone you might want to see here," he said.

I heard the voice before I saw him.

"Yo, Momma. Do you believe this? We just got here. You alright?"

I looked at my son and then leaned against the car, afraid to trust my legs to hold me up. It was Sydney who hugged me first, tightly and long, and whispered in my ear, "He's okay, we're all okay."

They were alive, but strangely, I didn't feel relief—only fear. It had been so close. And then they told me they'd been saved by milk.

"What?" I asked, unable to take in one more crazy thought. "What are you talking about?"

Paul laughed, but a giddy laugh, that let me know he'd been afraid, too. "We were talking to George. He has this concept for Greek fusion food and wanted our feedback. That's why we were going to go out with him this morning. To discuss it, taste a few things. Try his souvlaki breakfast tacos." He was babbling now, with relief.

Sydney took over. "I told George what we were doing in New York. He liked the idea of combining food you remember with what people eat now. We told him we'd bring cereal milk to breakfast, you know, to make the point? Anyway, George was running late, so we stopped at the store. We all got here just after the explosion."

I stared at them. I felt Darlene's hand on my arm and a take-it-easy squeeze.

"Why didn't you text me right away and let me know you were okay?" I asked my son. I was shaking now, not sure if it was from shock or anger.

"Gee, Mom, I was going to, but a lot was going on you know. A lot."

Before I could say something I would regret, George came up to us, his parents following closely behind him.

"It was a close call for sure. We're all lucky," George said. Beside him, Nick and Sophia looked years older than I'd ever seen them. I knew how they felt.

"Do they know what happened?" Darlene asked, trying to break the tension.

George ran a muscular hand through his black curly hair. "Looks like a fault with the propane tank. Maybe a leak? I haven't been out in the boat for a few weeks." He stopped and looked at the water, serious, absorbing the shock. "I'm thinking the propane collected down below and maybe the bilge pump set it off."

"Bilge pump?" Darlene asked. We knew what that was but had never heard of them causing trouble like this.

"Yeah," George said. "We had a lot of rain last night, and it would have collected in the bottom of the boat. The bilge pump's set on automatic to come on when that happens so the boat doesn't start to fill up." He shook his head. "Kind of glad it did. If I'd been on board and started the engine, I would have set it off myself...."

Nick took a step back and glared at his son, his worn face becoming darker and darker with rage.

"Propane? Did you say the propane tank was no good?" he asked, his voice rising.

He turned to address the crowd. "It's that guy who got arrested again. He delivered it. That Duck MacDonald, the one I sent to jail once already. He tried to kill George!"

CHAPTER SEVENTEEN

Sophia reached out and took her husband's arm, with an apologetic look to her son. "George, your dad's upset. We had such a bad, bad scare. We'll go home now, you come later," she said, leading a now deflated-looking Nick away to the car.

Officer Dawn Nolan came over to our group. We moved aside to make room and waited for her news.

"Alright, folks," she said. "It does look like a propane explosion; not much else it could be on a sailboat. We'll write a report. And George," she nodded to him, "the thing for you to do now is to contact your insurance company. In situations like this, they'll take it from here." She paused and looked directly at me. "The main thing is no one got hurt."

"Got the rain and the pump to thank for that, I guess," George said, his face serious. "I appreciate you coming out here so fast, officer. I'll make some calls. And you two," he said to Paul and Sydney, who seemed to have recovered from their near miss in a way that only the young and fearless can. "I still owe you a breakfast. My place? We need to get out of here."

"Agreed," Sydney said. "Paul, let's go."

"Sure thing." My son turned to me. "Terrible about the boat, eh? We'll talk to you later." He kissed my forehead. "You're the best."

Then, they were gone.

"You okay?" Darlene asked. "I have some of my old regulars coming in for some colors. If you need anything, you'll call, right?"

"Of course. You go," I reassured her. "I'll be fine. I think I'll go for a walk. I'm good."

I wasn't good, not at all, but at that moment, as shaky and in shock as I still was, I just wanted to be alone. Something had changed in me in the last few hours. I needed space to figure out what that was. I felt too alone for company. There was only one person I wanted now—my dad.

I went home and changed, then drove back to the woods to find him.

I knew the path, away from the water, into the trees, and up to the hills. This was where my father, Ed Rankin, used to take me on our walks. I would have given anything to be able to talk to him now. The truth was, when I was growing up, my dad was sometimes an embarrassment to me—other fathers worked on their cars or watched Hockey Night in Canada on Saturday nights, and my dad was a quiet Department of Natural Resources biologist—but no one was better at using nature to teach life's lessons. Always a scientist, never a hunter, my father would take me deep into the woods to teach me what he knew and, when it was dark, point to the stars. If he were here now, I would ask what I should do, but he wasn't. He'd been gone for over ten years, passing on soon after we lost my mother. Colleen, who'd stood for my mom at the wedding, said he had died from a broken heart. That had bothered me a lot at the time. I wanted to say, what about me, Dad, what about my heart? It had taken me years to forgive him and to understand Colleen had tried to comfort me by reminding me of how much love had been in our house.

I thought about families and how they remember. I thought of Catherine's old aunts, still not speaking over a disposed-of Featherweight sewing machine. I thought about Duck and the family who had predetermined his life so that even now, he was the first suspect when a murder was committed.

How well did I know Duck? How did that legacy make him feel? How much did he resent it? I looked at the scrubby spruce trees around me for answers, but they seemed to be waiting for me to tell them.

What did my dad say when I told him my teenage troubles so many years ago? *Look at the other side, Valerie. There's always another point of view.*

He was right. I stood still on the rutted, muddy track. I had been looking at this backward.

Maybe it wasn't Duck who was resentful but his family, with his chronically crooked, unable to think or be straight, small-time hustler brothers. His brothers who, when they were done crashing their cars, fighting behind the rink, trying a little arson here and a weekend breaking-and-entering there, had graduated themselves into the bad forgery business. His brothers who had gone to jail when their guileless sibling had told the police where he had gotten the bills. His brothers who had had lots of time to brood on that betrayal while sitting in their cells.

And what else would have been on their minds? What had happened when they were no longer able to operate the tiny rural empire of threats and intimidation they had built up over the years? Had someone moved in and tried to take over? And could that someone have been Wally?

It wasn't a stretch. Wally had tried to get a kickback from me, and he had likely tried the same thing elsewhere. Was that what this was all about? Had he crossed the MacDonalds and moved in on their turf? Was that why he was dead?

I tried to remember that day. The store had been busy; so many people had come and gone that afternoon. I had a mental image of the back parking lot and Wally's small bus, the door and back hatch open. Anybody could have slipped out and gone to the rear of it, touching nothing. *Hey, Wally, come here, got a question.* Had Wally walked down between the seats and gotten his throat cut?

Two birds with one stone, something my father the nature lover never let me say.

Wally taken is care of, and Duck is blamed for it.

Never forget what you did. The note in Duck's pocket.

Revenge.

Duck, blood on his hands and a knife in his jacket. Silent and resigned in the back of the cruiser as he was driven away. Help me, he'd said to me, but maybe not in defense but in despair. He knew he was off to prison again and knew who would be waiting for him there.

But the brothers weren't done—bullies never are.

Mr. Kosoulas.

The MacDonalds would blame him, too. A man who had the first dollar he had earned taped on the wall behind the cash register would notice every bill. And he did. How to get even? What was the worst they could do?

I knew the answer.

Hurt his kid. Sabotage his son's boat, that would show him.

It all made sense. Perfect, horrible sense.

The wind picked up and moved the tops of the trees. I was cold, in my bones, in my blood.

Up to now, maybe all my life, I had held back. What could someone like me do?

I thought of the smoke in the sky and how it had drifted away. I thought of how the world had nearly ended when I had thought Paul was gone. How could I ever be the same again?

I turned to go and headed down the hill.

Suddenly, in the periphery of my vision, I caught a movement, long-legged, fast and easy, keeping pace with me. Then, it moved past, ahead, turning in a slow arc to head me off.

Anxiety, even worse because of the day, came over me in a flush. What should I do? Stand still? Hide?

I went forward cautiously to the last bend until the logging track came into view. It wasn't far to the path and the road below. I was almost there. Then, something emerged from the bush onto the trail, maybe fifty feet from where I was.

I stopped.

A coyote. Tall and lean, still not recovered from the winter, a few patches of winter coat hanging from the bony flanks.

The animal stopped, and so did I.

We both stood and looked at each other for a long, sharp moment. I knew two things— that I was very afraid and that I wasn't. I felt something like a wave go between us, this animal and me. This is real, I thought. This is real.

The coyote's eyes looked straight at me and, it felt, right through me to the other side. It watched and waited.

My dad's counsel came to me: Every part of this animal was a hunter. It was ready; it always was. I was being evaluated; I could feel it.

The animal in front of me seemed to make a decision. For a moment, I thought I saw recognition in those eyes, but then the coyote reeled the look back out through me and into itself. Then, it turned away, loping deep into the bush as skillfully as it has come.

I was alone again. And I knew what to do.

CHAPTER EIGHTEEN

I went back to the yacht club, but the RCMP cruisers were gone. Rats, it would be so much easier if I could talk to the Mounties now. I knew who had killed Wally and tried to harm George. That knowledge lay heavy in my chest like a burden, one I needed to put down or at least pass on.

I wanted someone with power and authority to take this over. Someone who could get to the MacDonald brothers, take them on, put them out of business, make them face the consequences, and, most of all, make sure they couldn't hurt anyone else again, not Duck, not George, and most definitely not my son and his girlfriend.

I went over to my car, got in, and headed to the causeway and Drummond. On the way over to the detachment, I composed my thoughts, clearer now that I had figured it all out. This was the only logical explanation for what had happened. By the time I pulled into the RCMP parking lot, it seemed to me likely that by now the Mounties themselves had come to the same conclusion.

I was relieved to see that both Wade and Nolan were in, but surprised when the officer at the front desk said Rollie was there, too, meeting in a room at the back. She took my name, told me to have a seat, and disappeared down a hall, her heavy boots loud on the highly polished linoleum tile floor.

I waited for about twenty minutes, but eventually, the officer returned to take me back to the room she had just left.

They were all there: Rollie, Wade, and Nolan, at a long, battered table, scarred wood on the top, curved green metal legs nicked with scratches below, marked where they had been bumped by chairs over the years during many interrogations.

I said the first thing that came into my mind before I could catch myself.

"Rollie, why are you here? Shouldn't you be at the store, working? What's going on?"

"Just following up," Rollie said, as if that was an explanation, and as if that made sense.

Wade cut us off. "What can we do for you today, Ms. Rankin?" he asked. "Is this about that incident with the boat? We're happy no one was hurt, and it's now up to the insurance investigators to handle this. That should set your mind at rest."

No one offered a seat, but I pulled up a chair from near the door and sat down.

"Look, this may not be news to you, and if it isn't, just stop me. I figured it out," I said.

Nolan looked puzzled, Wade looked blank, and Rollie seemed wary.

"Figured what out?" Wade asked. "The boat? It was likely just a propane tank malfunction, happens all the time."

"No, not that," I said. "That's part of it, but I mean the bigger picture. Who killed Wally. Why Duck's innocent and the real reason the boat blew up."

Nolan pulled a pad of paper and pen toward her. Good, she was taking me seriously. Rollie looked at the ceiling.

I had to start at the beginning and explain it in order, chronologically.

"It's like the Featherweight," I began. "Family feuds, you know."

Rollie seemed to relax.

"Duck getting caught by Mr. Kosoulas was the reason all the MacDonald boys ended up in jail. We all know that." I looked around the room, trying to assess the response.

"The way I see it, they have been sitting in their cells or wherever you keep them, stewing about that and plotting revenge. On Duck for being Duck and such a lousy criminal that they all got caught, and on Mr. Kosoulas for catching him. Plus," I had another thought, "I am sure they weren't too happy with Duck being on the outside while they are still stuck inside, behind bars. That's got to be wearing on them."

Wade made eye contact with Nolan and Rollie.

"I assume there is a point to all of this, Valerie," he said, "apart from your observations on relationships inside the MacDonald clan."

Did I have to spell it out?

"It's obvious," I said, speaking rapidly now because I had so much ground to cover. "Wally was a small-time crook like the MacDonalds were, or are. He tried to shake me down and was probably pulling the same with a lot of people around here. Gasper's Cove and Drummond are where the MacDonalds operated, or tried to, in their way." I stopped to take a breath. "As I see it, they somehow took Wally out." All the time I spent watching crime series while I knitted socks was paying off. "And to cover their tracks, pinned the blame on Duck, to get even with him. You have the note. It was from them, warning him they were going to get him."

I looked at the three faces in front of me. "And today, with the boat, they were behind it, they had to be. They rigged that boat to blow up, to either kill George or hurt him to punish Mr. Kosoulas for catching the fake bills."

They all relaxed. I didn't understand—I had just delivered the punch line, brought it all together. Solved a crime, several crimes, for them.

Wade looked at Rollie.

"You first?"

"Why? Because I'm a relative?" he said. "Thanks." He leaned forward, his hands clasped over his knees, and looked at me.

I waited.

"Val, go home."

"What? Rollie, everything I said makes perfect sense, you know it does." My cousin was a smart man, why was he doing this?

"Valerie, you have no idea what you are talking about, none at all. You've had a shock today; I understand you thought Paul was on that boat. That's enough to make it hard for anyone to think straight. I understand the stress, we all do," he said, looking around the room. Wade didn't look like he understood very much. Nolan looked annoyed, ready to get back to work.

"But what other reasonable explanation is there for everything that happened? Tell me," I demanded.

"There's nothing to tell," Wade said, standing up, opening the door, and letting me know it was time to leave. "Today was an unfortunate accident, that's all. That piece of paper you found when you were snooping could have been from anyone, it's circumstantial. You're connecting the dots, but you're off the page. Yes, Wally was killed, and we have a suspect in custody." He opened the door wider and moved his face closer, so I wouldn't miss what he had to say to me.

"Coming in here with all this"—Wade paused, searching for the right word—"with all this nonsense is just not helpful, and in a small town, gossip like this is dangerous."

Gossip? Gossip? I was outraged. I thought of the coyote. I was a hunter, too. I had figured it out, couldn't they see that?

"Listen, I don't want to tell anyone in this room how to do their job, but it looks like I have to." I could talk slowly, too, make them listen. "Go check on the oldest MacDonald boys, they'll be running it, up to no good, from prison. You'll see I'm right."

"Valerie, where have you been?" Wade asked me. "If you mean big brother Clyde MacDonald? He's in Halifax, getting ready for a liver transplant. One brother's down there because he's a match, and the other guy, last I heard, had been born again, as a Hare Krishna. Not much of a criminal gang."

I stood in the doorway, half in, half out, and felt myself sink right there in front of the bunch of them, any credibility

I thought I had dripping down to the floor where it lay in a pool.

"Poor guy," I said. "Hope things turn out," I added, not sure if I was referring to the one with the bad liver or the one who was chanting.

I looked at the faces in the room. I saw various degrees of intolerance for me.

"I may be wrong about this, but I know I am right about Duck. If this didn't prove it, something will." Nolan and Rollie both stood up, ready for my exit. I waited for someone to say something, but when no one did, I filled the gap. "I guess I will be going now. Got things to do at home," I said, walking out into the hall. There was something else I had to say. "But I'm not done. I'll be back."

Wade started to close the door behind me. "Take your time," he said, shaking his head.

I stood still in the hallway. I wasn't ready to face the officer who had led me here. I was sure she'd hear soon enough that I'd made a fool of myself.

I was surprised at how I felt. I expected to feel defeated now, and embarrassed, but I didn't. Instead, I felt stubborn, almost strong; the setback made me more determined to carry on. What was happening to me?

This wasn't over. I was so tired of secrets. I'd interrupted something in that room. What was Rollie doing with the RCMP? Why wouldn't he tell me?

CHAPTER NINETEEN

I sat in my car in the detachment's parking lot, put my head on the steering wheel, and tried to think. I didn't know what to do next. Rollie was still in there, doing whatever he was doing, and I was annoyed. Where was his sense of responsibility? As far as I could tell, no one was, literally, minding the store. That seemed to be up to me. I put my key in the ignition and headed out. I'd pick up Toby and make it down the hill in time for opening at 10:00. I'd deal with my cousin later.

When my dog and I got to Front Street, I was surprised to see Colleen waiting at the locked front door of the store. She was all done up, Colleen-style, pink purse, purple top and pants, a pink scarf looped around her neck, and pink and purple beaded earrings, which she had no doubt made herself, dangling from her ears. Darlene called her mother the Queen of Matching. She wasn't wrong.

"You're here early," I said, rummaging in my purse for the keys. "Need something?" I pushed open the big doors and reached over to turn on the lights.

Colleen bent down to pat Toby. "No, Joyce Smith called me. Said to tell you she can't come in today to help in the Co-op. Her grandchildren are down with some bug. She has to stay home with them so her daughter-in-law can work. So I came. I know what to do."

"Appreciate it," I said. "Let me get settled, and I'll come up and show you how to do the cash."

Colleen stood up straighter and tightened the bow of the scarf around her neck. She looked offended. "No need. Don't you remember I worked here before I was married? That cash register and I are old friends."

I thought back. That was over forty years ago, and how long did she work for us? Two, three years maybe, before Rory whisked her off to a life of matrimony, maternity, and mayhem on a lane off the Shore Road?

"Of course, how could I forget?" I said. "You go to it, and if you have any questions, shout. This will give me a chance to take care of things downstairs."

Colleen smiled, and suddenly she looked younger; I could see Darlene in her. "Go about your business," she said. "I know what I'm doing."

Grateful for the help, I walked Toby to his post in the recliner near the front door and got started. Rollie had been mostly on his own the last few days, and the place was a mess. I gathered up empty boxes he'd left in the middle of the floor when unpacking new stock and took them to the back landing. I'd break them up and put them in the recycling later.

After about an hour, during which I sold paint thinner, potting soil, and plumbing parts to men who knew what they were looking for, Rollie appeared. Catherine was with him, neat and tidy in a pressed denim skirt and pastel striped sweater dragged down on one shoulder by the heavy tote bag sliding down her arm.

"Nice of you to drop by," I said, in no mood to be polite. "Finished your chitchat with your law enforcement buddies?" I nodded to Catherine but wished she wasn't there. If Rollie and I had been alone, we would have had a good old Rankin argument—it had been a while since we'd done that—and I could have found out what he was up to. But with Catherine standing between us, I had to hold my tongue. It nearly killed me.

Rollie ignored my attitude, which felt the same as if he were ignoring me. "I had some business to take care of," he said with excessive nonchalance. "Catherine's here to pick up a few things from the office, then I'll be out front to help you." I noted he neglected to thank me for doing his job for him.

"You do that," I said. "I'll be here, at the counter. Taking care of customers. It's been a busy morning," I added, although this wasn't true. Learning which elbow joints went under a kitchen sink hadn't exactly run me off my feet, but not being here, Rollie wouldn't know that.

My cousin studied me with a knowing look, as if I were a patient and not a relative, then took Catherine's elbow and steered her to the manager's office. As they passed me, Catherine reached across the counter, picked up one of the road maps, and smiled at Rollie, as if assuming he were going to give her the friends and family discount.

I picked up more garbage in a huff and carried it to the back, making sure to bang the empty boxes against the wall as I passed the now-closed office door. Since when were tête-à-têtes between those two on the agenda?

Stomping around the back landing, I picked up the cardboard cartons and began to pull them apart, flattening them for the recycling bin. I stopped. The logo on one looked familiar.

I looked closer. Next to the company name was a label "12-count Sensitivities limited ingredient grain-free pollock pâté." Shadow's food. Why was the box here? Had Duck brought in a case from home? I turned the box upright and saw a shipping label:

> ### KENNETH MCQUARRIE
> **73 Rosedale Avenue**
> **Gasper's Cove, Nova Scotia B2Z AO1**

What? Why was a cat-suspicious, bird-loving building inspector buying cat food, and, more specifically, the only kind eaten by the cat he had just met at my house?

I dropped the box and pulled out my phone. With nervous fingers, I scrolled through my recent calls until I found Kenny's number. I dialed.

He picked up immediately on the first ring, again. The man had a social life like mine.

"McQuarrie here."

"Kenny, it's Val. I'm here at the store. I know this seems like a weird reason for a call, but there's a cat-food carton here with your name on it." I struggled to come up with a reason why a label on a cardboard box warranted a call. "Since I have a cat staying with me now, I was just wondering where you ordered it," I added, aware this sounded as lame as it was.

There was a long pause. No doubt Kenny was trying to decide whom he should call to report I had lost my marbles.

"Oh, that," he finally said. "I left it at the store for Duck a few weeks ago. It was Polly's idea. I have always wanted to do something to repay him for rescuing Max. When I saw him with that cat, I knew she was right. He'd appreciate it."

A spark went off in my brain. I swallowed.

"Did you by any chance leave a note with this box?" I asked. "One that said *Never forget what you did*?"

"Yeah, sounds about right," Kenny said. "Why?"

"Oh, just found it, wondered if I should keep it," I lied. Departing from the truth seemed to be my new skill.

"Right," Kenny said. I could hear the doubt. "How are your blue jays?"

"Grown and flown," I told him. "I am pretty sure I see them around the neighborhood."

"Probably you do. Don't be surprised if you find eggs in that nest next year. Long memories, those birds. They know where they're safe."

"I hope you are right," I said. "Thanks for your help."

"No problem," Kenny said, chuckling. "Anytime. Boxes or birds."

I hung up the phone and looked out the small window of the landing to the parking lot, where not long ago a murder had been committed. I'd worked hard trying to figure out why, and so far, all I'd done was entertain the RCMP and solve the great mystery of who had bought a box of sustainable pollock cat food.

Good work, Valerie. I looked at the clock. It was almost 3:30. Polly would be here soon, and she could help Rollie, assuming he decided to come back to work. Then, Toby and I could go up the hill to the safety of the house. I'd had enough excitement for one day.

When we were finally at home, I located the cat, asleep in the laundry hamper in the basement, and started dinner. Too tired for much of an effort, I pulled some chicken out of the fridge, cut some onions, squash, carrots, and peppers, and shook it all onto a baking tray. I poured olive oil over the chicken and vegetables, added some salt, pepper, garlic, and oregano, and turned the oven on to heat it up. The lazy cook's standby, sheet-pan dinner. That would do it. I'd have a hot dinner, turn on the TV, put my feet up, drink tea, eat the leftover chocolate cake I'd found at the back of the freezer, and spend the evening pretending life made sense.

That was just what I needed, and just what I did. After the animals and I settled in, Shadow on the back of the chair behind me and Toby at my feet, I picked up the remote and looked for something distracting to watch.

It wasn't easy. I didn't want to watch anything for mature audiences only, or with scenes of violence, or cartoons. That didn't leave much. However, *Plundering the Empire* caught my eye. The title sounded historic, and that reminded me of Stuart, so I clicked and started watching.

I forgot the cake. The story in front of me, the true story, was riveting. I had no idea how many museums and art galleries around the world still held art, artifacts, jewels, and valuables taken illegally by successive colonial empires—French, Spanish, Italian, Dutch, and British—from the countries they had occupied. Sitting there in my modern living room with my dog and my cat, I was shocked by the extent of the plunder, the looting, and the theft. Some countries, such as Greece, had whole government departments devoted to finding Ancient Greek treasures and bringing them home. Where had I heard of this before? Of course, Mr. Kosoulas and his newspaper—the ring recovered from a private collection here in Canada.

I pressed pause and sat up to think. My mind was whirling, my ideas spinning so fast they were almost ahead of my thoughts. This made perfect sense. The parachute. Whom could I talk to? Who would understand?

I picked up my phone.

"Stuart? It's Valerie Rankin. Do you have CBC GEM, you know, the streaming service?"

CHAPTER TWENTY

I'd been to Stuart and Erin's house once before to pick up an order of friendship bracelets the girls had made. It was a bungalow like mine, probably built around the late 1950s like mine, but, unlike mine, had been completely renovated, which, given Stuart's profession, was no surprise.

I'd put on some lipstick and thrown on a coat after he'd answered my call and said, "Sure, do you want to come over?"

For an awful moment, standing there on his front steps, I wondered what I'd do—or, more precisely, what I would feel—if Kimberly were here, too. It was a school night, not a date night, but not knowing the nature of the relationship, I wasn't sure if weeknights made a difference. In all my years as a single mother, I hadn't dated. I had no idea how these things worked.

Erin opened the door. Past her, into the kitchen, I could see Stuart at the sink, a towel over his shoulder. As far as I could tell, only the two of them were home.

Erin looked at me and smiled. I could see her new braces. Taller, fairer, and less serious than Polly, Erin was the creative side of their partnership. Her use of color, even on something as simple as a woven bracelet, was interesting and, to my eye, sophisticated. She also had an offbeat sense of humor that I was sure was not as appreciated, or as useful, in junior high as it would be in later life.

"Hey, Valerie, you got the bag I left for you at the store? Polly gave me a production deadline, I just made it," she asked.

"Yes, I did," I said. I took in the sight of a kid at home, in her sweatshirt and leggings, loose socks on her feet. It wasn't that long ago my own children were this age. How nice it was to be so young and so secure, a parent doing the dishes, homework done, time on your hands, no place you had to be. How nice it was to be the parent, in the last few years of a world in which you could provide everything your children needed or wanted.

Stuart heard me and walked from the kitchen to the door, wiping his hands on a tea towel. He wore an apron and had clogs on his stockinged feet.

"Come in, come in. Your call intrigued me. I found the program you talked about. What do you want to show me?" he asked.

"Would you watch the beginning of this series with me?" I asked. "I know it sounds insane, but I want to know if you have the same reaction to it as I did." I hesitated, but I knew this was the clincher. "I think it might have something to do with Operation Fish."

Stuart's head snapped up when I mentioned the obsession his father had passed on to him. "Operation Fish?" He stood aside and pointed to the living room and the big-screen TV mounted on the wall. "Have a seat, I'll bring in tea."

Erin smirked at me slightly and followed her father into the kitchen, and I turned to the couch. Although our two houses had been built about the same time, inside they couldn't have been more different. In contrast to the vintage splendor I'd inherited from Aunt Dot, Stuart's house was new, modern, tasteful, and what Darlene would call curated. A large teak ceiling fan shaped like a propeller hung from the ceiling above a rough linen couch with corduroy pillows. The coffee table was a stump of wood, beautifully grained and polished, carefully stacked with granite coasters. There were floor-to-ceiling bookshelves of birch, a sleek turntable for what appeared to be an extensive vinyl collection, and many, many plants. In some of the pots, I saw little dials like meat thermometers to tell Stuart when the soil needed moisture. A beautiful guitar leaned against the wall in the corner.

I sat down on the couch, which was deep with a low back and nearly swallowed me up. From my vantage point, half sitting and half lying on his furniture, I looked up to see Stuart handing me a mug of tea.

"My apologies," he said. "It's just Earl Grey. I should have asked—would you rather have herbal? Chamomile? Rooibos? Milk? Sugar?"

I sipped the tea—it was hot, and the pottery mug was heavy.

"No, this is great, thank you. Lovely house."

Stuart looked around the room as if he hadn't noticed it before. "Erin and I are sort of homebodies; I guess we like to be comfortable." He picked up the remote. "Let's turn this on and see what's got you so interested." He put his tea down on the wooden stump and sat beside me.

Side by side, we settled in and watched the documentary about treasures stolen and taken away by colonial powers who'd never considered that it wasn't their right. I was very aware of Stuart beside me, and for much of the show, I found myself watching his face as much as the screen. I could tell he had the same reaction to the story, the information, and its revelations as I had had.

When the program was over and after we watched the credits roll by, Stuart let out a whistle. "They were worse than pirates, those guys. Who did they think they were? Museums and private collections. It was all stolen."

"Exactly," I said, putting my mug down next to his. "Treasure, priceless treasure, and it all belonged to other countries, other governments. No wonder they want it back."

Stuart looked at me. "I think I know where you're going with this," he said. "You think artifacts like these, from collectors, from museums, were part of the cargo on the HMS *Emerald*, don't you?"

This was one sharp guy. Finally, someone who didn't need to be convinced that I had some ideas that made sense.

"You got it," I said. "I came here to see if you think that could have happened. I mean, the parachute, that maybe it came from that ship, somehow, some way, at some time. My question to you: Is there any way that some of these valuables made their way to these shores, too? I know it's far-fetched, but that parachute, I can't get it out of my mind. It is trying to tell us something."

Stuart's mouth went into a firm line, and I could tell he was thinking. He sat there for a long time until his thoughts were interrupted by the sound of water running in the kitchen.

"Young lady," he called out. "It's time you got ready for bed. You have school tomorrow, it's late. Go. Now."

I heard the fridge door open and Erin's muffled voice from behind the door. "Dad, chill. Just getting a snack. I'm going, I'm going."

Stuart waited until Erin appeared, with a plate and a glass of milk and headed down the hall.

"Brush your teeth," he called after her, then turned to me. "Back to Operation Fish. Stay where you are, I have something to show you."

Stuart got up and headed down the hall. He returned with a copy of his father's manuscript.

"Something you said rang a bell, something my dad once told me. Let's see if it's still here."

I sat and watched as he began to leaf through the papers. He knew them well and found what he was looking for.

"I knew it, look here," he said, holding a page out to me. On the thin sheet in his hand, meticulously typed many years ago on a manual typewriter, I could see notes handwritten in the margins, in pencil. I couldn't read what was written, but I could make out a series of large question marks. Had Stuart's father written this?

"I remember him talking about it," Stuart said, with growing excitement in his voice. "It was just rumors, he could never verify it, but after the war, some of the seamen talked about some things taken from the cargo by a couple of the boys hidden on board somewhere, never found, never recovered. Nothing ever turned up or was reported missing. No way to know if the story was true."

Stuart and I looked at each other, an idea that passed between us stronger than words.

"Not many places to hide things on a ship...," Stuart began.

I finished his sentence for him. "Except maybe on deck, stowed away on a seaplane."

"Are you suggesting what I think you are?"

"Yes, I am. What if the parachute wasn't the only thing the storm brought ashore? What if there was something else, something so valuable it was worth killing for, that ended up here, too? What if that's what Wally was looking for, why he wandered around the coast? *All who wander are not lost.* That's what it means."

I saw the puzzled look on Stuart's face. "A bumper sticker. Forget about it. Well, now I know what we have to do."

"And that is?" Stuart asked.

"Exactly what at least one other person is trying to do," I answered. "Find the *Fairyfox* and the treasure she brought to this coast."

CHAPTER TWENTY-ONE

For a moment, Stuart looked excited, but then skeptical. The historical romantic his dad raised had been replaced by the engineer.

"How do you think you're going to do that?" Stuart asked. "The island's not that big, and there are more than enough people already looking around the coast."

This got my attention. "Like who?"

"Think about it. Wally, the tourists, seasonal residents, and real estate folks. Nova Scotia has been discovered. If there were remnants of an old plane or a treasure, you'd think it would be found by now. Even Kimberly has me driving around all the backroads, it's nuts."

Kimberly? Not the direction I thought this conversation was going to go, but I was interested. "Driving around, what do you mean?"

Stuart sighed. "To tell you the truth, I felt like I'd answered one of those ads in the paper."

He lost me. "The paper?"

"You know the ones, *Wanted to meet. A nice senior gentleman with a car.*"

I laughed. I was sure Aunt Dot had placed that ad before Florida called.

"Not sure what's going on," Stuart continued. "She came by the office one day and asked me about some of the renovations I'd done on houses in the area. Next thing I know, I am in the car driving her around to see them, then it was jogging, and now yoga." He stopped and looked at me, confiding in an old friend. "Do you have any idea how bad my hip flexors are?"

"Probably about the same as mine." It was all I could think of to say.

Stuart looked uncomfortable. "I'm sorry, I don't know why I shared that. It's been a long day. But you still haven't told me how you are going to find something that may or may not exist along this coast, decades after it may or may not have been washed ashore."

I stood up and picked up my purse. It had been a long day for me, too. Stuart had no idea how long.

"By not looking for it, that's how," I said. Something James had said to me suddenly made sense—be available for information, let it come to you. "I'm not looking for a treasure," I said. "I'm looking for the treasure hunter. I'll come up with a plan."

I went home. Thanks to the birds, I had her number. Even though it felt odd, I bypassed my son and went direct.

> Hi. It's Valerie. Paul's mom. How
> are you?

Great.

I have a favor to ask. I need your
digital skills.

Of course. Anything.

Can I meet you tomorrow for lunch?
Or are you done with Greek food?

No way, going to be there anyway. Tasting for
George. Can we do it early instead? Before they
open?

Perfect. Appreciate this.

No prob. I'll tell George. See U there.

There, I'd done it. I had a feeling Paul would be annoyed
with me but pushed that thought aside. I had things to do
and needed someone who could do them. He'd cope.

The next morning, I was at the restaurant very early, but
the kids were already there. George saw me through the
window and got up from the booth where he, Sydney, and
Paul appeared to be sampling from small plates, and let
me in.

My son looked up, smiled, and pushed a plate toward me.
"Hey, Mom, have a seat. George is doing amazing things."
He used his fork to identify the food for me. "Gyros lasagna,
sushi in grape leaves, souvlaki breakfast tacos, of course."
He raised a glass. "And this is a tzatziki smoothie. Loaded
with antioxidants."

"Where's your father?" I asked George. Nick the conservative was probably passed out on the floor in the kitchen with a stroke.

George laughed, knowing why I'd asked. "The week's been hard on him; he'll be in before lunch. I tried to tell him not to worry. The insurance is going to come through, and the boat was old anyway, but he won't listen." He looked up at me. I realized I had never seen him sit down in the restaurant before. "I'm going to give him a few days until I tell him what I'm going to do."

"This is the best part, an awesome idea," my son interrupted.

George was pleased with the praise. "Keep it to yourself, but I'm going to buy a food truck. Greek fusion food. These two figure I'd kill it during the tourist season."

"Absolutely," Sydney said, then seemed to remember my texts. "Was there something you wanted to talk to me about?" she asked.

"There is," I said, "but why don't we move to another table and I can tell you about it? I don't want to interrupt the tasting."

Paul looked at me with suspicion. "What's this about, Mom?"

"Oh, nothing, just a surprise. For your birthday. Won't take long."

Sydney gave me a puzzled look but took my cue. "Yeah, that's it, Babe, your mom and I have to talk about something."

Sydney and I moved to a booth at the back and sat down.

"Okay, what's this about?" she asked. Very business-like, this one.

I pulled out my phone. I'd been up half the night working and doing research, finding the right pictures. I leaned over so she could see and started scrolling.

"What I am wondering is, given your technical expertise, would it be possible to take this picture of a necklace I made"—I showed her the one I'd done, laid out on the dining table at home, gaps along the stringing cord carefully left bare—"and these pictures of beads from museums"—I held the phone closer to her—"and sort of put them together so it looked like the old beads were on this necklace?"

Sydney looked up from the phone and right into my eyes. "Can I ask why you want to do this?" No fool either, this girl.

I searched for a reason that would sound more plausible than the reality. "For marketing," I said, channeling Polly. "A campaign we are doing for the Co-op. What do you think?"

The look on Sydney's face said she thought her boyfriend's mother was a liar, but she seemed willing to let it pass. "Sure, I can do it, no problem. Just send me the images," she said. "Might be interesting. When do you need this?"

"Whenever you can." I paused. "And I wouldn't mind it if you kept this to yourself. Paul's birthday, remember? We'll have to talk about that, too."

"Definitely," Sydney said. She got up, gave me a long look, and walked down to join the fusion tasters at the table. I waved as I went by and let myself out.

Things were happening.

I sat at my kitchen table and looked at my muffin tin full of recycled beads. I got up, walked down the hall to the bedroom, and lifted the lid of the jewelry box on the dresser. I pulled the necklace out and held it to the light.

It was one of the first necklaces I'd made. Polly had put a picture of it on the welcome page of the online store. Like all my necklaces, I'd composed it by feel and sight, slipping beads on and off in no particular order until they looked right to me, familiar.

What made this necklace special was the leaves. Delicate, veined, and long, the leaves had tiny holes on the stems perfect for beading. I'd put a few of them at the front, almost like a medallion.

Classic, that's how it looked—classic.

This wasn't a surprise since I'd seen leaves almost exactly like them on a screen last night, from the Hellenic period 250 BC, in a museum in New York.

I'd started this chain of events myself. I was sure of it. Now, it was up to me to stop it. A necklace I'd made had gotten the attention of someone, somewhere. Had it been me who had lured a treasure hunter, a murderer, a blower-up of boats here to Gasper's Cove?

There was only one way to find out.

CHAPTER TWENTY-THREE

Sydney worked quickly, and she was good. The images she sent me the next morning looked, to my eye, like a completely unaltered photograph of a necklace someone had made with old beads, some of them two thousand years old, from a muffin tin on her dining room table.

Perfect.

I went to work. Polly had shown me how to upload items for sale to the Co-op website, and I did that now. I considered the price and decided to go high:

$49.99

I typed, then added,

Going fast.

Pick-up only.

Contact 902-555-0100.

Satisfied by how clever I was, I pressed "Save."
My trap was live.

I made a cup of tea and waited. Since I had already attracted a lethal treasure hunter to Gasper's Cove with a picture of one of my creations, I figured it wouldn't take long for that person to contact me again. Five minutes passed, then twenty, then an hour.

After a time, Shadow jumped up onto the kitchen counter and, with great delicacy, began to bat my phone to the edge, making the point that a watched phone never rings.

"You're right," I told her. "I need to distract myself." I had a sewing session to think about, the last drop-in, UFO (unfinished project) Saturday of the month. I liked to use these meetings to float ideas for new classes.

What did my students want? What had they asked for? I remembered—fancy dresses, proms and bridal, slow projects that would require new techniques, fitting, and fabrics before the end of spring.

We'd have to talk fabric, synthetic and natural, polyester and silk. Silk. The parachute. How fun would it be if I showed up with it and told the war bride's wedding dress story? They'd love it. I caught the phone just before Shadow sent it flying and called the library.

Catherine was in.

"Hi, this is Valerie. I wanted to call and apologize if I was a bit short with you in the store the other day. It was the morning George's boat blew up, my son was supposed to be on it... my nerves got the best of me."

"Listen, no need to apologize," Catherine said. "Rollie told me all about it. I felt terrible for you. How are you doing now?"

I looked at my phone. Where was our abrupt and efficient librarian? Who'd replaced her with this sympathetic confidant?

"Better now, thanks, trying to get back to normal," I said, thinking that this was true if you considered trying to smoke out a homicidal maniac a normal activity. "Right now, I'm getting some of my sewing classes ready. I have a favor to ask."

"Anything for you," Catherine said. This was getting weird. What was going on? I remembered the brown women's cardigan hanging on the hook in Rollie's office. Was he giving Catherine therapy? Was that it?

"It's about the parachute. I'm thinking of pitching the idea of a class on bridal wear to my students and thought it might be a conversation starter. If you still have it, can I borrow it? I promise to be careful," I added.

"Bridal wear?" Catherine made a noise that almost sounded like a giggle. It couldn't have been. "Of course. The Archives said we could keep it; they already have seven in Halifax. I've been doing research for a display here. When do you want it?"

I had to get out of the house. "How about if I come in this morning? Is that too soon?"

"No, that would be perfect," Catherine said. "I'll get it folded up for you and print off some relevant information. I am sure your ladies would be interested."

As soon as I arrived at the library, one of the senior volunteers rushed over to meet me.

"Catherine said to bring you back," he said, waiting for me to shake the rain from my umbrella and lean it against the stand near the door. "Come this way," he said, hustling ahead of me like a waiter leading me to the best table, pleated pants close to his armpits, new velcro sneakers on his feet. As we worked our way through the stacks, my guide stopped every now and then to push errant books back neatly into place in their rows, until he delivered me to the old boardroom. Inside, Catherine stood at a long oak table, the parachute laid out carefully in front of her, a stack of neatly stapled photocopies in a pile beside her.

"I'm pleased you asked for this," she said. "The research I've done on this project has been thrilling, that's the only word for it."

I studied the librarian. Something was up. Catherine had clips in her hair and her cheeks were pink. Blusher? And was that mascara? The brown cardigan was on the back of a heavy oak chair.

"Thrilling?" I asked. "In what way?"

"Sit down," Catherine ordered, a hint of her former self in her voice. "Let me show you. I've been reading about the Chute Girls—young women who worked during WWII in Winnipeg, Saskatchewan, and all across the country, packing parachutes. The Air Force thought the work was too tedious for men." She snorted. "Can you imagine what those girls had to put up with?"

I could.

"Look at this," she said, pushing a reprint of an old newspaper article to me. "A Canadian woman, G. D. Martineau, wrote this. She called it *The Parachute Packer's Prayer.*"

I read it out loud: "'Today I'm a Parachute Packer, And my heart takes a turn with each fold.'" The poem went on to describe the young woman's care and responsibility, but it was the last lines that got to me:

Give my heroes kind wind and fair weather.

Let no parachute sidle or slump,

For today we go warring together

And my soul will be there at the jump.[2]

"Wow," I said. "Who knew?"

Catherine's eyes were bright. "I know, they were amazing, weren't they? And what they did wasn't easy. I have been practicing for two weeks." Her hands smoothed the silk on the table in front of us. "Now, what we have here doesn't have the harness or cords anymore, but I've been reading. It was fifty-six square yards of fabric, and even still they could fold it into a package about a foot square."

"Amazing, but that's silk, it disappears to almost nothing," I said. "But how did they do it?"

This was the question she'd been waiting for.

"Like this," she said, her hands quickly folding the large square into accordion pleats, back and forth. "Of course, it would be bulkier with the gear on it, all that's left are a couple of the D rings, but look at how small it is." She held up a neat, tight package. "Take this and show your students, but make sure you tell them the story." She stuffed the

---

2. Elinor Florence, "Cheers to the Chute Girls," *East Kootenay News Online Weekly (e-KNOW)*, *www.e-know.ca > regions > cranbrook > cheers-to-the-chute-girls*

photocopies into a large library envelope and passed them to me with the silk.

I laid the papers down and took the parachute from her, honored and touched to have it entrusted to me. "I'll be careful, but it's raining. I don't want to get the fabric wet."

Catherine reached for a thin plastic bag, then looked at my large raincoat. "You didn't bring a bag. Do you have an inside pocket in that thing? Just to be safe, keep it dry?"

"Of course," I said, opening my coat to show her my large dog leash pocket on the left side. We slid the compact package inside and zipped it closed.

"There," I said, "it should be safe. I'll get this back to you as soon as I can, and I will tell you what my students think."

Catherine beamed as she opened the door to the boardroom as I left. There was something about her, a sense of frustration in her own untapped resources, a waiting for a chance, that I had not seen before. I'd make sure my students appreciated the work that she'd done.

On my way to the front of the library, I stopped to read some of the notes Catherine had given me, but before I could, my phone buzzed in the welt pocket on the front of my coat.

I tried to stop my hands from shaking as I pulled out my phone.

Unknown caller.

Love the necklace, want to see it. Where did you
get the beads? Are there any more?

Oh, no. I hadn't thought ahead this far. For some reason, I thought they'd show themselves, not ask to see me. Where was I going to meet this person, this treasure-hunting murderer? Where would I be safe? It had to be around people and plausible. Not at the Co-op, it was too isolated up there on the second floor.

> More?

I asked, trying to buy time, then I had an idea.

> The beads came from the Recreate and Recycle Depot in Drummond. How about later? Meet me there at 5:00?

A nice public place.

Perfect. My mind caught up with what I had just done. Now, all I had to do was explain all this to Annette and call the RCMP. I was finally getting somewhere.

CHAPTER TWENTY-FOUR

Annette's face under the bangs she'd cut herself, a little short, looked confused.

"Can you go over this again?" she asked. We were in a quiet aisle at Recreate and Recycle, and I was explaining my master plan. "You have set up a meeting with a buyer for a necklace that doesn't really exist? Here, in my Depot? The one I manage? Can you tell me again why? That's the part I'm not getting."

I started again, giving Annette the high points of my scheme. "Okay. I made a couple of necklaces from beads I got here. It's a long story, but I think some of those beads were extremely old and valuable. It's sort of a lost treasure situation. Anyway, we put a picture of one of those necklaces on the Co-op website."

"I get that part, so far so good. We can talk about where the beads came from later. But the rest of it, about Wally... well you lost me there."

"Of course. It's a lot. But this is what I think happened. My necklace, those beads, attracted a treasure hunter. I think

162

that person was someone Wally either drove around or ran into when he was lost. In either case, my feeling is that Wally saw something, and he was killed for it." Annette's face was a mask. This conversation was a long way from craft supply odds and ends and Tupperware.

I plowed on. "The way I see it, the only other person who thinks about ancient treasures is Mr. Kosoulas, because he always sees things from the Greek angle. So, of course, this treasure hunter blew up George's boat." Annette's eyes went wide. "Now, they are on the hunt for our jewelry. Plus, they stole the earrings James left in his car."

Annette turned away from me and started to pick up some Barbie clothes that had fallen onto the floor. As she stuffed tiny sheaths and stiletto shoes back into a bag, she contemplated my theory.

"Got to tell you, this sounds way too complicated to me," she said, repositioning the bag of Barbie outfits on a peg on the wall. "But then again, a lot of really weird stuff has been happening. There has to be a reason for it, that's for sure."

I handed her a tiny pillbox hat that had dropped on the floor. "Look, Annette, there is a dangerous person out there. I think I am the one who brought them here," I said. "And I feel responsible to make sure they are stopped. Does that make sense?"

Annette thought it over. "I guess it does, but just so I understand what you're saying, you think if a necklace brought them to Gasper's Cove, a necklace will catch them? Is that right?"

"Couldn't have said it better myself," I said, which was true.

Annette held up a hand. "Okay, that's the part I want to talk about, before you go any further. What's going to happen when they show up?" she asked. "Who's going to catch this treasure-hunting killer? You and me?"

"Yes."

"Are you telling me you invited a homicidal maniac to my place of work, without asking me?" Annette didn't look too happy about this.

"I didn't think you'd mind."

"I do mind. This whole thing sounds crazy, but on the off chance you're right about this person, I don't want them here. Have you called the RCMP?"

"I did. Sort of. The woman on the phone wouldn't put me through, but I made her promise she'd pass on the message."

"I'm afraid to ask. What was the message?"

"I said to tell Wade we needed backup at 5:00 at the Recycle Depot. Be discreet. I thought that was important to say."

Annette pulled over a chair from the end of the aisle, moved a bag of children's craft scissors off it, and sat down. She looked tired.

"Val, you're a friend, a good customer, and an excellent sewing teacher. Usually, you make sense. Not now. But in the tiny, very tiny, chance you might be right about this, I'll wait with you until the RCMP gets here, and let's hope that's before the killer shows up. I didn't have a lot of time for Wally, but he didn't deserve what happened, and that thing with the boat, if it wasn't an accident, that's not good at all. What do you want me to do?"

This was more like it.

"Watch the entrances," I said. "I'm going to go out and stand by the car so they'll see me. I need you to keep an eye on the back door, just in case."

"Can't be too hard," said Annette. "I have things to sort out there anyway. But one more question. Who are you expecting to show up? Any ideas?"

I'd thought about this, and the list was long. "I figure it has to be someone from away. So, anyone who isn't from Gasper's Cove, I guess."

Annette stood up and looked at me. "Valerie, you do realize that nearly the whole world isn't from Gasper's Cove, don't you? That doesn't narrow it down much."

"You're right," I said. "That's why it's going to take two of us. You know me, Annette. I never give up."

Annette stared at me for longer than was comfortable, nodded as if this made sense, and walked off to the rear of the building. I went out the big glass door to the parking lot out front and started waiting.

I stood beside my car; the rain thankfully had stopped. Then, the late afternoon sun came out, and the day became humid. I took off my coat and threw it into the car. I walked around the parking lot, making myself visible to any approaching cars, read the community notices taped to the front window of Recreate and Recycle, and ambled around the perimeter of the lot in a system, once walking around in a big circle to the left, then around another to the right.

I watched the occasional vehicle go by, waved to the people I knew, and stared at the people I didn't. A few regulars went in and out of the store, and I chatted with them a bit. Someone pulled in, dropped off garbage bags in the donation bin, and then left, ignoring me. I read texts Annette sent me from her post at the back of the store.

No news yet

I wrote back at least six times.

At 5:37, I started to panic. No mysterious antiquities buyer had shown up. Had I scared them off?

Then, it hit me. I was an idiot.

Why did I think that the treasure-hunting murderer would wait for 5:00 to see me, like I was an appointment at the dentist? Toby and I had watched enough police procedurals to know the criminals always cased the joint. Whoever I had attracted was probably already here and had likely been here before I had arrived. I thought of the interior of the store, of the crowded aisles, crammed with bins of orphaned knitting needles and rotary cutters, safety latches broken. I thought of the stacks of stained-glass scraps, and I wondered where the dagger was that belonged in the voodoo knife holder.

The Depot was a warren of so many places to hide. All the killer had to do was to go in, look around for the beads, wait for me, and attack.

Except I wasn't in there. Annette was. She, as manager, would know more than anyone where the beads were now and where they had come from. What had I done?

I pulled out my phone and texted her.

GO INTO THE BATHROOM NOW
AND LOCK THE DOOR!

Minutes passed.

What? Why?

I remembered how slowly Annette moved.

Do it! Killer there. Hide. Be safe.

In here now. Help!

Where was Wade, the RCMP? The officer I'd left the message with was the same one who had shown me out the last time I was at the detachment. Was it possible she hadn't taken me seriously and done nothing?

What could I do?

Dawn Nolan.

I had her direct number, from some business that had happened last year. I called it, and she answered.

"Officer Nolan here."

"It's Valerie Rankin. Get to the Recreate and Recycle Depot as fast you can. The murderer is here, I'm afraid they're going to get Annette."

"Hold on," Nolan said. "The murderer? What are you talking about?"

"I don't know who it is yet, but I know why they're here looking around the coast. I did something, and the person contacted me, said they'd meet me here. Now, they're here, and Annette's in there with them. Get here fast!"

"On our way."

I didn't know what I should do next. If Annette was locked in the bathroom, she might be safe for the time being. The RCMP would arrive soon, but I couldn't just stand here; I had to draw the killer away from Annette.

Something my father had shown me on one of our walks flashed into my head. A kildeer, a kind of plover, limping toward us along the shore, noisy, wings spread out. The nest is near, my dad said. She's trying to draw us away from it.

That's what I had to do now. I reached into my pocket and pulled out the tissue-wrapped package. Inside was the original necklace, the one from my jewelry box, the one from the website. I pulled it out and spread it to swing in my hand, like a display, or a taunt.

I opened the door of the Drummond Recreate and Recycle Depot and went in to find a killer.

CHAPTER TWENTY-FIVE

I hadn't gone far, only past the scrapbooking supplies, when I heard the siren.

Oh no, they'll scare the killer away. I ran through the door. The siren went silent. Officer Nolan, Wade, and Rollie stepped out of the cruiser.

"Annette's locked in the bathroom," I yelled. "Go get her before it's too late!"

The two officers rushed past me and into the Depot, leaving me alone with my cousin outside.

"What are you doing here?" I asked Rollie. "Are joining the RCMP now?" I was glad to see him but didn't want to say it.

"I was there when the call came in. I know you; I thought I should be here," he said. "Do you want to tell me what's going on?"

I told him. I told him everything, about Operation Fish and the *Fairyfox*. About the parachute and about Stuart's dad. I held up my necklace and told him about the beads and about how someone had stolen the earrings I gave James. I told him why I thought Wally was killed and why George's boat was blown up. Then, I told him about the trap I had set and the message I got back. And finally, I told him how I'd left Annette alone and at risk.

Rollie listened. I was relieved to see him finally take me seriously. "Stay outside, Valerie," he said, pulling the door open, careful not to let me follow. "Stay here and don't move."

I did what I was told and waited and worried about Annette. Because I couldn't think of what else to do, I resumed my patrol around the parking lot and, for the second time that evening, hoped for an end to this nightmare.

Finally, Rollie, Officer Nolan, and Wade came out of the store. Annette was with them.

"Had to break into the bathroom to get her out," Nolan said. "What did you tell her?"

"The killer," Annette's round face was flushed. "The killer, did you catch them?"

"Can't say we found anyone in there who shouldn't be there," Wade said. "But I have to ask, do people really pay good money for bags of old corks and puzzle pieces?"

"You'd be surprised," Annette said. She turned to Nolan. "So, no killer?"

"No, and I can't say I'm surprised," Nolan said, looking at me.

I was offended. Was this how our national police force worked? Couldn't they see that with their sirens and big heavy boots, they'd scared the treasure hunter away? We'd missed our chance, and it wasn't my fault.

I held up the necklace. "How about this?" I asked. "Evidence from the Hellenic Period, 250 BC. Whoever murdered Wally came looking to get more of this." I waved my jewelry in front of them. "How do you explain what I have right here, in front of you?"

Annette's eyes went wide as she reached for the necklace.

"You found them! Those leaves, the beads. They are from the Autumn Splendor Collection. Avon, 1964." She fingered the strand with reverence. "My mom had the whole set: necklace, brooch, clip-on earrings. Wore them all the time, they were her favorites."

She looked up at me, and I saw there were tears in her eyes. "I saved the earrings and the brooch, but the necklace was broken, and I thought I'd lost it. These beads and the leaves are part of it, must have gotten mixed in with everything else when we donated her old jewelry."

Everyone looked at me. I'd outdone myself completely this time and had nothing to say. The awkward silence went on for far too long and was broken only when Colleen came out through the doors of the Depot.

"There you are, Valerie. Darlene made me get a new phone, and I wasn't sure if I was doing this texting thing right," she said, sounding relieved, but paused when she saw the RCMP cruiser and the two officers. "Am I interrupting anything?" she asked, turning to me. "I thought we were going to meet, and you'd show me where you found those beads, you know, for my earrings?"

My legs wobbled, and I leaned against the hood of my car. I felt tired, very, very tired.

How clever, some scheme. All I had done was reel in Colleen, whom I saw all the time anyway, with the promise of ancient jewels, sold by Avon only a few decades ago. I felt sick.

Then, I had another thought, one that made me feel even worse.

Sydney.

My home-for-only-a-short-time son's new girlfriend. She'd find out how I'd made a fool of myself and dragged her into it. She'd think I was a complete lunatic. Just as bad, I had, by association, embarrassed my son. How was I ever going to make up lost ground like that? I'd blown it.

Wade had no such worries. "That's it, then," Wade said. "Rollie, over to you. This better be the last time."

"It will. Count on it," Rollie called out as the two officers strode off. He turned to me. "Let's go back now, Val. It's time we had a chat about a lot of things."

Rollie was silent on the trip across the causeway, down Front Street, and into the store. Once inside, he marched me past Polly and a customer without even acknowledging them and down into his office. I felt like I was being taken to the principal's at school.

In the office, he pulled out two chairs and closed the door. He didn't offer me tea.

"Sit," he said. "That was a fiasco over there. Can you tell me what has you so involved with this? Why you can't let it go, why you are making such a fool of yourself and of our whole family? Explain yourself."

"Explain myself? How about you? Where do I start?" I'd had enough. "I don't know who you are right now, but you're not acting like anyone related to me."

Rollie's face went red above his beard. Here we go, I thought, a big old Rankin argument about to launch. It was about time. "What do you mean?" he sputtered.

"I mean the secrets. Hanging around the police station like it's normal and I'm not supposed to notice. Not being worried enough about Duck. And Catherine, something's going on there. She's wearing makeup. Being sweet. It's creepy." Rollie looked offended, but I kept on going. "You aren't telling me anything, and in our family, we tell each other everything. This is not how we operate." I paused for dramatic effect, pleased with how this was going. "Then, there's the really big thing you won't tell me."

"What's that?"

"The parachute!" I was shouting now. "Annette said Duck brought it in with a bag of drop cloths. Where would he get a thing like that? Tell me."

Rollie sighed. "I guess you have a right to know. Given everything, it's time."

"Time for what?" I suddenly realized I wasn't prepared for whatever was coming next.

"You know the book James is writing?"

"Yes, of course." Where did that one come from? What was he talking about?

"The diary he is using as a primary source. It came from us."

"Us?" What did he mean, *us*?

"Yes, us. I felt it was time we got the real story out. It's not just our history, we don't own it. But I didn't know how. I had to find a way that didn't implicate the family or our reputation."

None of this was making any sense to me. "I have no idea what you're trying to say. Out with it."

Rollie looked at me, annoyed, but continued. "James gave me a way. I knew he was frustrated with how the book was going and that he had difficulty with sources, so I approached him. He agreed to use the diary for his research but tell his publishers it had been written by "Anonymous." Worry crossed his face. "I hope I haven't exposed him to risk, asking him to do that for us."

It made sense now, why James had been so evasive about the diary's origins. It hadn't come from Colleen at all. It had come from my own family.

"You're telling me we were the rumrunners? The Rankins?"

"Not exactly rumrunners, but we helped them, and in some ways, you could say we ran with them. It was something the men in the family knew about, and when those operations stopped, there was no point in talking about it anymore."

The men knew? My mind was reeling. Here I was, a Nova Scotia mafia princess my whole life, and I hadn't even known it. I leaned back in my chair, unusually almost at a loss for words—but not quite.

"I've always been proud to be a Rankin, so this is hard to take in. You're saying we were a bunch of criminals?"

"It was more complicated than that," Rollie said. "You have to think of the times. This was an insignificant place, a place the world, the country, and even the province forgot about, if it ever knew it existed. It was a hard, hard place to live. It was just us here, with the wind, rocks, the sea, and the fish. Our family just did what all families did here—we survived."

"You're making excuses, romanticizing what went on," I said. "It was still illegal. What exactly did we do?"

Rollie started to speak, not only to me but also to our ancestors, in their defense. "It was complicated," he said. "We didn't just sell ropes, nets, and salt. We supplied provisions to rumrunners so they could outrun the law in both Canadian and American waters. We let them dock here on dark nights on our wharf and stow away cargo. It was all so they could provide for their families. We were just like the bootlegger who took a man's wages and then gave most of it back to his wife, or like the local police officer who shut the bootlegger down but allowed him to open again every now and then so he could earn enough to pay the fines. In those days, laws got broken, but only because we were honest."

I knew what Rollie was trying to do, but he lost me. All I could see in all of this was that they'd lied to me, my whole family had lied to me, my whole life. Why did Rollie know all this, and I didn't? I knew the answer, and I hated it.

"But I still don't get it. How did this never come out before?" I asked. "Why wasn't anyone ever caught?"

Rollie shrugged. "Let's just say that our family and the men they worked with were never proven guilty, but they were never proven innocent either," he said. "It was like that in those days."

I saw it then. "And the best way to hide an illegal business is inside a legal one, isn't it?" I asked him. "The better our reputation, the safer we were. But the parachute, you blew me off when I asked you before."

Rollie was caught off guard. "That? I found it when we were cleaning up downstairs, around the same time I found the diary. Just like I told you, I thought it was an old sheet, and I threw it into the pile and told Duck to get rid of it. I had no idea what it was or that he'd taken it over to the Depot."

Something flickered in my mind.

"I could still be right, couldn't I?" I asked Rollie. "If the parachute made its way here because of some rum-running comings and goings, how would we know that something else from the *Fairyfox* isn't around out there?"

Rollie stared at me. "Don't start with that nonsense again. Let that fantasy go." He was annoyed now. "And this whole crusade you've got going about Duck, leave it alone. Let things play out. After all the drama, your credibility is shot anyway." He looked less irritated now and more concerned. "And another thing. If there's something dangerous going on, I want you out of it, for your own safety. Is that clear?"

I nodded, but Rollie had no idea. The men in the family were not the only ones with secrets.

CHAPTER TWENTY-SIX

I stood in my kitchen and watched my animals eat. I'd make my own dinner later; I was too upset to think about food now. What a mess this all was. So many big ideas, so many leaps off the cliff of logic, and so many theories about the parachute, the treasure, and secret activity along the coast. I had suspected everyone but myself, my own family.

And I'd lied, or maybe not lied, but held back.

I had told no one what Duck had said to me that day, that he'd asked me for help.

Why? Because I couldn't do it? Because they might think I was the last person who could?

So far, they'd be right about that.

But I couldn't let it go. Duck deserved a chance, and he deserved a defender, probably a better one than I was, but I was the best he could get. It was as simple as that.

Nothing was settled, whatever anyone tried to tell me. I knew it. There were still too many ends untied, too many threads unclipped. Sure, up to now I'd gotten most of it wrong, but who had it right?

What was I to do with all these facts, not ideas, things I knew were real but didn't add up? I was exhausted with Rollie holding back about the RCMP. I remembered that Catherine had read Stuart's dad's papers, and she'd picked up a map. I knew that Kimberly wanted to be driven around the coast and that Jennifer Fox, the cooking imposter, was on Wally's tour, as was Sydney, the friend who'd wanted to come to Nova Scotia.

A bowl banged on the floor, and I looked down. Toby had stepped aside, and Shadow was carefully picking her way through the last of the food in his bowl. The dog looked up at me with joy in his huge brown eyes; he'd made a friend, a connection.

Why wasn't my life that simple? I turned on the faucet to fill the kettle for tea and looked out the kitchen window. The nest was now empty; the babies had flown away. Wistfully, I reached for a cup, and as I did, I noticed the calendar from the Agapi on the wall next to the cupboard. George had done a good job; the pictures were amazing. I turned the pages— January, February, March—and looked at the intimate views of the coast taken from his boat, all documenting the rough beauty of the edges of Gasper's Island. I had never studied the place from this perspective, with this eye. I'd missed so much.

George hadn't.

He'd captured the coast in all seasons and at all times of day: just before daybreak, morning, midday, evening, and night. I flipped the pages through the rest of the year, then noticed something. Two boats, unfamiliar to me, neither local fishing dories nor leisure craft, appeared in September and October, half hidden by rocks on the far side of the island, one in the early morning, one close to dusk.

I stopped, the cupboard door open, the cup in my hand.

What had George captured with his camera? Something he shouldn't have? Had George, like Wally, witnessed a crime?

I put the cup down. Shadow jumped up on the counter and held out a paw to me. Touched by her trust, I stroked her and thought.

Maybe the watched had been watching. I had to find George and talk to him. I called the restaurant.

"He's not here," Mr. Kosoulas said. "He's gone off to see your kid and that girl with the tattoos everyplace. Busy here, too. Want a job?"

"Not at the moment," I said. "Got my hands full. But thanks for the offer." Mr. Kosoulas grunted and hung up.

Paul and Sydney. I hadn't heard from either of them since before the triumph of my murderer reveal at Recreate and Recycle Depot. That made me uneasy. I knew Gasper's Cove, and by now someone, or even everyone, would have told them what had happened. There was no point in putting off the conversation. I texted my son.

How are you doing?

Mom. Sydney told me you had her work on that image. Not cool.

I'm sorry Paul it was just an idea.
Didn't work out.

We need to have a conversation about boundaries. Got to set some now.

Boundaries?

I felt like I was going to be sick.

Yeah. I think space would be good for everybody.

Listen can we talk about this? I am so
so sorry.

Just got in. Waves were good. Got to go. Leaving
for NYC soon.

We need to talk.

I stood in my kitchen and waited. I tried again.
A new notice.

Notifications silenced.

I went to the kitchen chair and sat down. What had I
done? When was Paul leaving? Would he go without seeing
me? I had to do something.

I looked at the clock on the stove. Soon, the sun would go
down. If Paul was in from surfing, he'd be at Noah's place
now. I had to talk to him, face to face. This text-message
business was not going to work. I had to straighten this
out and fast. I bent down to pick up Toby's bowl and then
reached for the coat I'd thrown on a chair. I'd give the dog a
fast after-dinner walk around the block and then leave. I'd
drive out, talk to Paul, and apologize to Sydney. I'd fix this.

I'd hoped the drive out to see my son would make me
feel better, but it didn't. Instead, all I felt was the nausea of
shame. I opened the car window to let the cold air blow in,
but that didn't help. What had come over me? Why had I
gotten so caught up in this imaginary investigation? Why
had I done so much I now regretted? The RCMP thought I

was a nuisance; Annette and Colleen thought I was crazy. The men in my life were all mad at me, too, or at least Rollie and Paul were, and I was sure Stuart wouldn't think much of me either when he heard what I'd done. Stuart had trusted me with the legacy of his father's research, and I had used Operation Fish to make a fool of us both.

The drive became as dark as I felt. The wind blew heavy gray clouds over the sky and shut the last of the sun out, and I had to turn on my lights to see the road along the coast. Beyond the ditch, the trees bent as the wind picked up. It wouldn't take me long to get to Noah's; there were no other vehicles on the road.

Except one.

Out past town, just after the turn to the look-off, a large black truck passed me going the other way. It flickered its lights briefly, the universal sign for lower your high beams, but I checked, and mine weren't on. The wind blew, and a tiny purple cardboard square, my 50–50 ticket, lifted from the dashboard and flew out the window, triggering a memory. Rumrunners, matching two halves of a bill. The big roll on a table in the church basement. The ticket in Duck's pocket.

I reached down and rolled the window up, just in time to see lights flicker in my rearview mirror. The black truck. It had passed me, taken a U-turn in the parking lot of the look-off, and turned around and come back. I was being followed.

Yes, it was her truck.

Annette.

My seatbelt felt tight against my chest. How stupid was I? It was right there in front of me all along, but I had gone off on some romantic, crafty, wild goose chase instead. There were no treasure hunters, just local smugglers, evading taxes and hurting no one but governments like they'd always done, coming into hidden coves only they knew, and George had recorded. Quite the operation, organized by quite the operator. Someone who did a little bit of this and a little bit of that, making ends meet because every little bit counts. Someone at the Co-op the day Wally was killed, someone whose dad was a plumber and could meddle with a propane tank. Annette. Sitting at the table in a church basement, selling tickets, driving all over the island, making her deliveries. Was that what happened? Had Wally the hustler found out what was going on and tried to cut in?

And what had I said to her? I'd never give up.

That was definitely Annette behind me now in her truck, two, no, maybe only one turn behind me.

I needed help, but how? If I called the Mounties, would they ever find me in time? I needed to get off the road and find somewhere safe. But where? Noah's place, where Paul and Sydney were, was at least fifteen minutes ahead. I had to find a house, someone to take me in.

The logging road. I knew it. I made a hard turn off the highway, left the pavement, and went onto the dirt road. I turned off the lights, parked, and got out. I was Ed Rankin's daughter, and I knew where I was. Down the end of this road to the left was the path where we used to go blueberry picking. If I followed that down, I would be on the rocky beach, the one where the summer homes were. If I could get there and find someone, I would be safe.

I heard a truck behind me brake and then turn. She'd found me. I ran to the ditch and the culvert under the turn to the Shore Road, jumped down, and lay flat. I heard a door slam and a voice call out.

"Valerie? Are you okay? It's me, Annette. We have to talk. I have to explain something. I hope you won't be upset. We can work it out. Where are you?"

I stayed where I was. I pressed my face hard into the grass, and sadness rippled through me as I thought of my animals. This is what Toby would do. If I can't see you, you can't see me.

Annette waited and then called out again.

"Whatever. I guess you need privacy," she muttered to herself. "Catch you later," she called out. I heard her feet stumble and then walk back to the truck. The engine revved up, and then the truck pulled out, turned, and drove off, the sound fading as it headed back to town. Carefully, I stood up. There was grass in my hair and mud on my coat. I looked far down the road and saw the truck swerve, pull into the look-off, and stop.

What was she doing? Waiting for me to show myself so she could follow me again? I wanted badly to drive off down to see Paul and Sydney, but I couldn't lead her to them.

What next? I didn't dare get back into my car and turn the lights on or go near the road. I could only continue, go down to the beach, and find someone to help. Not much of a plan, but the only one I had. I started out.

I walked carefully along the dark path, using the flashlight on my phone to see. Once on the beach, it was easier—I could hear the surf to my right and see the lights on in one house to my left, the front of the building cutting into the wind like a ship.

James would help me.

CHAPTER TWENTY-SEVEN

As I walked, the wind blew the clouds away, and the moon came out. It was almost full, high and bright, in the sky. A ripple of reflected light shimmered below it on the dark ocean water. As I climbed the steps toward the modern house, I suddenly felt the whisper of my ancestors beside me, and it was a comfort. This is what you saw, I thought, this is where you were, these are the waves you heard. Now, I'm here.

I wondered about them, the women and men who had lived on this island generations ago, and who had had the sense to be humbled by it. They knew the secret dips in the rocks at the bottom of the cliffs, they knew the paths, now mostly grown over, like the ones that had brought me here. Perhaps that's where they had walked down to meet the small wooden boats sent ashore from the rumrunners' ships.

Were those memories, hidden in me, why I couldn't let go? Maybe that was why I kept searching for the *Fairyfox*.

Who was the Rankin who found the parachute after a storm and took it home? Maybe only the sea knew now.

The house above me called like a sanctuary. I had a friend there. The top of the stairs was close to the large deck, next to the bushes along the path to the driveway at the road side of the house. Walking along it, I passed an open garbage bin, wine bottles lined up beside it, a bakery box, and the small package I had delivered with the earrings visible at the top.

Suddenly, the whole lawn down the slope to the rock wall that separated the property from the beach below was flooded with light. Up on the cantilevered deck, high above the water, the huge lighthouse lantern went on. It rotated slowly, as it was designed to do, sending beams of information to someone out there—a working light now and not a piece of patio art. Frozen, as if the light were a searchlight for me, I looked up. Then, as abruptly as it went on, the huge light went out, its job done. I turned and looked out at the ocean. There, I could make out the running lights of a boat, and above them, another light blinked. Message received. I stepped back into the bushes and tried to think. I was confused, but my instinct spoke to me.

I wasn't safe here. Not at all.

Not knowing quite why, I felt my body panic. I started to jog, past the unlit stairs up to the house, past the door to the garage, so I could get closer to the road and away.

But before I could reach the mailbox at the turnoff to the Shore Road, I heard a voice behind me.

"Stop!" I'd been seen after all.

Like a fool, I turned around, and then I was done. A bright flashlight shone into my eyes, and I raised a hand to try to stop the blinding glare. From under the visor of my hand,

I looked over and saw James Martin, professor emeritus, with a flashlight in one hand illuminating his face like a pumpkin at Halloween, lit from within, but with eyes that were flat, dull like a fish on a deck of a boat. In the other hand, he held an old-fashioned revolver.

"Up the stairs," he ordered, jerking his head toward the steps up to the deck. "Now."

I had never seen a gun before, not in a hand, and not up close. With wary steps, I walked past him, smelling the scent of aftershave and wine, and climbed to the big deck above.

When we were both there, he pointed with the gun. "To the railing, go."

I went as he asked, past the big light right to the edge of the deck, put my hand on the railing, and looked out. I heard the surf, I saw the moon, and I smelled the sea. Calm settled over me. I belonged here, this man didn't. Turning around, my hands tight on the railing behind me, I looked at this polished, polite, and deadly man. I heard my mother's voice in my mind. "Honestly, Valerie. You just have to have the last word, don't you?" Not wrong, Mom, not wrong.

"So, James, this is your next move?" I asked. "Kill me because I saw it and figured it out? The light, it's your signal, so they know when to come ashore." James was still, the gun in his hand more steady than I would have liked. "It's kept you busy, hasn't it? Covering your tracks. Wally, Duck, and George." The man's face made me very angry now; my son could have died. "Anyone could figure it out, and this nobody did."

"Ha!" James said, his lips curling back, his good looks gone. "Why didn't you stick to your knitting? You have no finesse."

"Finesse? You have no idea what I do," I said wildly. "You have to buy clothes, I can make my own. And those croissants? You got them at the store, I found the box. And the earrings, no one stole them, did they?"

James stepped back as if I had pushed him. I'd caught him off guard.

"You went through my garbage?"

"You should recycle," I shouted, all self-control gone. "All those bottles. And you know what? You have to stop killing people, framing them for murder, and blowing up Greek men's boats."

For a brief moment, the flashlight wavered, and I saw something flicker across the professor's face. James Martin, criminal mastermind and rumrunner wannabe, was a little bit nervous now, maybe even afraid.

I'd found my edge. I was someone's crazy mother—there was nothing more dangerous than that.

The gun moved and then went steady again. I knew I was going to die, so I leaned against the railing and looked up into the night sky.

I saw the Big Dipper.

I knew so much more than this man, and I'd figured him out. "You didn't want to study the rumrunners, did you?" I accused him. "You wanted to be them. You thought you could come into this community and put on its history. But you know what?" I couldn't stop now; I was speaking to both of us. "You can't have anyone else's life; you only have the one that belongs to you. The only primary material is yourself."

Sorry, Mom. Now, he's going to kill me.

The wind came up again, climbing the cliff and coming onshore. I heard the rattle of the cord against the metal flagpole beside the house. Good wind for sailing, I thought.

I slid my hand into my double-entry welt pocket, past the lining and into the big pocket inside my coat. It was still there, wrapped tight and small as only fine silk can be, light, strong, and undetectable. My fingers went to work, feeling along the ridges of the flat-felled seams, until I found the hem and touched a D ring. Circling my fingers through the metal half-circle, I pulled my arm out of my pocket as fast and as wide as I could and trusted the wind, my wind, our wind.

For a moment, the parachute flapped long and flat like a sheet on the line, then the air caught it and it rose, a giant round shape, 420 denier, tight in the wind, opening up in circle like a spinnaker on a boat, snapping in the night like a tablecloth in a church hall. Open and wide it spread, the fluted folds made by female hands releasing. Like a giant chrysanthemum, it left me and moved toward James, a giant fabric hand, that reached for him and wrapped around him so tightly that he lurched past me and fell over the edge where the manicured lawn ended and over the edge down to the rocks and water below. Then, it released him to the night and to the ocean, letting him go, delivering him down before it lifted again, and then, like a white ghost on a gust, floated away out to sea, alone.

The soul of the sea, returning at last, the way that she'd come.

CHAPTER TWENTY-EIGHT

I stood there on the deck for a long, long time, not looking down. I stood there until I was cold, until I heard the sound of tires on the gravel of the driveway, the sound of doors slamming and voices calling my name.

The stairs shook as they all climbed to see me. I turned around, and the first face I saw was Annette's.

"Geez Louise, Valerie, what are you trying to do to us? I found your car, but I couldn't find you, so I called the Mounties. We have been searching everywhere. This was the only place where anyone was home."

Dawn Nolan moved forward, walked past me to the railing, and shone a light below. She turned to Wade and nodded. They both left us and went down, passing Jennifer and Kimberly as they came up the stairs.

Jennifer? Kimberly? What were they doing here?

"U.S. Customs." Jennifer put out a hand. I wasn't sure if it was to greet or to steady me. "We've known there was a smuggling operation based out of here since the summer. I've been undercover working with my Canadian counterpart." She gestured to Kimberly, who now looked very serious and much less perky.

"That's right," Kimberly said. "George Kosoulas talked to us, and we had our suspicions about Martin. When Annette called..."

I was in shock. Annette came over and put her arm around me. "How did you know?" I asked Jennifer. Annette and I needed to know. "What was he smuggling?"

"Organizing the smuggling, you mean. The usual. Cigarettes coming up from the U.S., Canadian whiskey going down, evading taxes and duties."

Wade returned up the stairs. He paused and looked around at the group on the deck, then settled on me. "Valerie, we'll need a statement. How about you come with us?"

I was expecting this, but for a brief, fleeting moment had an image of Duck and the last time I had seen him. What did all of this mean? Why was he still in custody?

"Perfect," I said, as inappropriate as that sounded. "I have some questions for you, too." Wade might have thought I'd missed his jaw clench, but I didn't. "But first, I have to ask Annette something."

"Sure," Annette said. "What do you want to know?"

"Why were you following me? What did you mean, you had to tell me something?"

"Right. I was out delivering an order, and when I looked at the numbers for the drawing, I saw I'd made a mistake. You'd won the seventeen-piece serving set, but I'd given it to someone else. I am so sorry, but I'll get another one for you. Is that okay?"

I nodded, but before Annette and I could discuss colors, Nolan had her hand on my arm.

"Can you ladies work this out at a later date?" she asked. "There's a dead body down on those rocks, in the water, and we need to talk to Valerie."

"No problem," Annette said as I was led away. "Canisters are on special this month," she called out. "We can talk."

I waved to her from the cruiser. New canisters would be nice; I needed to get that kitchen updated.

I spent the rest of the night with Wade and Nolan, going over all of it, why I was at the house, the gun, the croissants, and even the parachute. The gun interested them most. When we were done and they said I could go, I called Rollie. He arrived about fifteen minutes later but, to my surprise, didn't whisk me away but came into the interview room and sat down with us.

Rollie rubbed both hands over his face and then looked over at me.

"I owe you an explanation," he said, glancing at the two RCMP officers.

"Go ahead," Nolan said, as Wade looked at her in agreement. "No harm in telling her now."

I stared at both officers and then at my cousin.

"What's going on?"

Rollie reached over to pat my hand, but I pulled it away before he could. "First of all, I'm glad you're safe. I can't believe, given all we were doing, that we didn't figure this out sooner." He looked at Nolan and Wade. "I feel responsible for the risk you took there tonight."

It felt good to hear an apology, so I decided to leave it there and not share that I had been at James's house because I had thought I was being pursued by a murderous Tupperware lady. That, I would keep to myself, probably forever.

"Don't blame yourself," I said, partially meaning it. "But what about Duck? What's going on with him?"

Wade took over. "After we brought Duck in for questioning, for obvious reasons, Rollie came to see us. He'd recognized a man leaving the store, from his days in the prison system." I had an image. The man with the yellow hat, could that be him?

Rollie interrupted. "It happens now and then, I recognize someone I knew from the job," he explained. "It was a professional relationship, so my policy has always been to walk on by, to respect my former client's privacy. But that day, it was different. I knew who it was, I had to report it."

Wade looked grim. "We followed up and, fortunately, were able to pick this individual up. It was a hit alright, but he didn't know who'd hired him. That's when Officer Nolan had an idea."

I looked at Nolan. She leaned forward, coming into her own. "I, we, decided that the fastest way to get to who was behind Wally's murder, and the smuggling operation in the area, was to let it keep running, and"—she paused for a breath and looked pleased with herself—"the best way to do that was to have the ringleader think that framing Duck for the murder had worked. After all, why would we keep looking if we thought we already had someone in custody? And all your theories and wild goose chases about treasure hunters added another layer of distraction."

I decided to let the reference to me pass. "So, that was James's alibi? That the killer had been caught?" The two RCMP officers nodded. "And you let him keep thinking that so he would relax and go about his business?" The three faces around me looked serious. This was exactly what they'd done. "Where's Duck now? When is he coming home?"

"Where he's been doesn't matter," Wade said, "but he's on his way now."

I sat back in my chair. Something Stuart had said came to me. "The truth was protected by a bodyguard of liars?" I asked.

Rollie looked startled. "I wouldn't put it that way myself, but it's not wrong." He paused and seemed to assess me. "You've been through a lot tonight. Why don't we take you home?"

He walked toward the door, then stopped when he realized I was not following him. "You coming? What's going on?"

"Nothing," I said pushing the chair back. "Just thinking about a promise. In my own way, I kept it."

On the ride back to Gasper's, Rollie tried to make small talk and avoid real conversation. However, there was little chance of that with me in the car.

"George. Let's start with him," I said. "What did he tell the RCMP about James?"

"That's not for me to share. Let's say not all of George's pictures ended up on calendars," Rollie replied. "Can't we do this later? You've had quite a night."

"Not like the day you're going to have if you don't start telling me some things," I said. "Just so you know, your lifetime quota of keeping important information from this female cousin has been all used up. No renewals. Talk to me."

Rollie sighed. "What do you want to know?"

"The boat, how did James blow up the boat?

"That one's easy. He didn't. Saltwater, corrosion, an old tank, leaking slowly for a while. Propane is heavier than air, and after a few weeks, the smell dissipates. The propane was collecting in the hull, and all it took was a spark. George was undoubtedly right about the bilge pump."

I absorbed this, but I wasn't finished.

"Catherine. Let's talk about her. You know she was on my list." Rollie looked uncomfortable.

"What list?"

"One of the people who had an abnormal interest in the coast. She took a map. Why would anyone who lived here do that?" I asked. "I figured she might have been a treasure hunter because she wasn't herself. But maybe that's because of the therapy."

Rollie shot a look at me. "What therapy?"

"Her sweater, Rollie, I saw it in your office. And you only close the door when you are giving personal advice." Anyone who thought I didn't notice things was wrong.

"I guess now's as good a time as any...," Rollie started and let it trail off.

"Oh no," I said. I knew that voice. "You and Catherine are an item? Is that it?"

"Yes. I have never been happier by the way," Rollie said. "But we wanted to wait and tell you because... it has ramifications for you."

Got it.

That could only mean one thing. A dress. They wanted me to throw in a custom-made dress as a wedding present. Was Catherine going to go for white or ivory? With her coloring, I'd recommend ivory. Maybe pearls. Off-the-shoulder? I tried to remember what shape Catherine's shoulders were.

"The maps," Rollie continued, "are for us. We want to buy a place and run a bed-and-breakfast. We've been looking around. Catherine's got a razor-sharp business mind, and she can cook. And the best thing I do is host."

A bed-and breakfast? Was everyone going crazy? "Rollie, can you take that on? I mean, with the store? It's a lot." I was a little disappointed we weren't talking about a dress; I had a vision already. Pearls. At her age, she could carry off pearls.

"That's the thing, isn't it?" Rollie said. "I would leave the store." We were parked in my driveway. I could see Toby up on the couch, watching us through the front window. He must be desperate to go out.

"You can't do that! Close Rankin's? We are part of this community, we have such a history here, okay some of it illegal, but still a history. What would people do without us?"

"Please," Rollie sounded distressed. "Let's do this when we're not both exhausted."

"Forget that," I said. "I've just watched a man fall to his death, found out I've been fed a pack of lies, worried to death about a friend for no reason, and now you tell me you're closing the family business." All the stress of the last twenty-four hours poured out of me with my words, bouncing off the dashboard, careening between the windows, trapping Rollie where he had no choice but to answer me. "Why do you think you're here? You are Rankin's. There is no one else to run the business."

Rollie twisted in his seat, a large man in a small car, a mild man trapped with wild emotions. "That's where you're wrong," he said. "There's you."

CHAPTER TWENTY-NINE

I didn't sleep that night. How could I? When lay in my bed and closed my eyes, all I could see were faces. Wally, with his comb-over up in the wind. Duck, in the back seat of the RCMP cruiser, looking doomed. James, the scholar, but no gentleman, dead on the rocks. I also thought of Stuart and his dad, of bilge pumps, of earrings, of Winston Churchill, of coyotes, and of church-lady sandwiches. I thought of Colleen, who wanted to stay where she was, and Annette, who worked so hard so she wouldn't. I thought of my son and my own hopes handed to him, and of all the things a person can lose and can't get back.

I lay there in my bed, with my dog and the cat, until sometime very early, just before 7:00, my phone rang. It was Paul.

"Mom, are you okay? I can't believe it."

"I'm fine, don't worry."

"Are you sure? We're coming down the coast. Can we see you tonight?"

"How about dinner tomorrow? I have a few things to do, and I need to rest a bit today." The truth was, I wasn't sure I could get out of bed, much less get dressed. I struggled to sit up, and Shadow jumped up to lie on the pillow behind me. She started to lick the top of my head.

"Get it, but you're okay, right? Listen, if we come for dinner, Sydney has a request."

My heart sank; I was no New York cook. "What's that?"

"Tuna casserole? Her mom used to make it when she was a kid."

I smiled inside.

"Tell her she can have all she can eat. See you tomorrow night?"

"You got it. And Mom?"

"Yes, Paul."

"I love you."

"Love you, too."

I lay back in the bed, finding room on the pillow beside the cat. I felt better now I'd talked to Paul, but still numb, as if the fear of the night before still lingered in my bones. Would I ever feel normal again? I pulled up my duvet. I wondered how long I could hide before Toby wanted to go out. Somewhere under the blankets, my phone buzzed. I searched and found it. It was a text from Darlene.

OMG. Just heard. How are you?

Fine. No, not fine.

Imagine. Coming over.

No, no you don't have to do that.

The world wasn't going to let me stop.

I have to go the store first, how about lunch?

I got dressed and took Toby out. It felt strange to walk the familiar route around the block as if nothing had changed, when everything had. James had been alive at this time yesterday, and today he wasn't, and I had been that close to being killed myself. What was a person supposed to do the day after something like that?

I needed everything to slow down, and it wouldn't.

And then there was Rollie. There was no way I could take on the store. I knew it, and when his romance-softened head had firmed up again, my cousin would see that, too. I didn't have the skills, I didn't have the experience, and I didn't have the smallest bit of managerial ambition. I knew who I was—a small-town sewing instructor and crafter, the kind of person who worked for you, not someone you worked for. I just couldn't do it.

That was that.

Before this idea went any further, I had to straighten Rollie out. There had to be a way he could do both Rankin's and this thing with Catherine. We'd all help; we could make it work. I'd walk down to the store and plan what I'd say on the way. Surely, Rollie could see things were fine the way they were.

When I got to the store, I saw Polly at the front counter.

"Rollie? You just missed him. Slow Saturday, he went out for coffee, he'll be back soon."

"He left you by yourself?" This didn't seem right. "Is Mrs. Smith upstairs in the Co-op?"

"Nope," Polly said. "She called in, couldn't make it. She has to clean the house. Noah has decided to stay out at the Point. She says she wants to get the basement ready to rent."

"Really?" I perked up, an idea taking shape. I thought of Duck's lonely apartment. "Would she allow cats?" I asked "Small gray cats?"

Polly smiled. "I suppose you can ask," she said, and then stopped. "We have to talk."

"We do?"

"Yes. Definitely." Polly lifted the hinged end of the counter and came around to stand beside me. She'd grown, and we were almost eye to eye. "I know."

"Know about what?"

"Everything. Not just about yesterday. I know about how Rollie and Catherine are going into the hospitality industry. I know this place will be under new management, and that the new management is you."

"Rollie said that?" I was speechless. Who else had he told? This was getting out of hand. "That's not going to happen," I protested. "I am completely unqualified. I can't do it."

Polly held up her hand. "Stop. Look, self-doubt is a normal aspect of performance pressure. You wouldn't be a great leader if you didn't feel that now."

"Leader?"

"I know what you're thinking. Sure, there are HR issues, and the operational side needs an overhaul, but don't worry. I can help you."

"You can? With all due respect, I am a sewing teacher, and you are in junior high."

I had offended her.

"I think it is more appropriate to say in five short years, I will be in university, but that's beside the point. I have the experience."

"You do?"

"Listen, all the tax planning for my parent's real estate business? You're looking at her." Polly reached over and put a hand on each of my shoulders. "I can show you an accounting program that will change your life."

The thought of that alone terrified me. "But, Polly, I have never managed anything in my life."

My advisor rolled her eyes. "I get it, but you need to move past the start-up mentality. Look at what you've done. You've set up a hub of rural economic development upstairs at the Co-op, drawing on and maximizing the power and potential of grassroots production. Retooling a traditional business model for the twenty-first century is your next challenge."

"Do you think I could do it?" I asked her, and then regretted it.

"Not only do I think you can do it." Polly was gently shaking my shoulders now. "I don't think anyone else can." She let go of me, went back behind the counter, and returned with her backpack in her hands. "In fact, I had the prototype cards printed on the machine at school." She unzipped her bag and pulled out a small stack, secured with a hair elastic. She peeled off a card and handed one to me.

"Mine first. This is just the draft. I'm still working on the website and the mailing list provider."

I took the card and read.

POLLY HEIDI BROWN

BUSINESS STRATEGIST AND CONSULTANT

Visionary solutions to meet compelling customer-facing needs

Polly watched my face and then, satisfied, handed me a second card.

"This one's almost there. Rollie told me your middle name. I'm looking at quotes for printing the first two hundred."

Valerie Moira Rankin

CEO and Creative Director

Rankin's General Store
115 Front Street
Gasper's Cove, Nova Scotia

"I'm considering adding *A woman-run business*," she said. "On brand, what do you think?"

I looked at my corporate strategist and saw hope not just for me but also for herself. I gave up; I couldn't let either of us down.

I handed the card back. "Perfect. Add that woman-run thing on the bottom," I said, "and get a quote for one thousand—we're going to need them."

CHAPTER THIRTY

I looked at the card in my hand, but before I could say anything more, a customer arrived in search of a compression fitting for a water line. I had no idea what he was talking about, but Polly did. I left them to it and headed down toward the manager's office, a space that my whole life had been occupied by someone older, a man of the family.

I could hardly open the door. Rollie had started packing, evidence of his determination to leave, a decision that felt more inevitable now than it had a short day ago.

I surveyed the chaos. The desk, for the first time, was clear. Folders and receipts were stuffed into file boxes and books; a giant pair of rubber boots, a few unwashed mugs, and an extensive collection of snacks, previously well-hidden, were jammed into plastic shopping bags, presumably for the trip home or to the new B&B.

I went behind the desk and sat down. Rollie wasn't on any coffee run. I'd been set up—left to assume the management of the family business, briefed by a teenager. Most people seemed to think they knew me better than I knew myself.

There was a knock at the door. "Come in," I said.

It was Stuart. He walked in, careful to avoid the debris on the floor.

"Glad I caught you. I wanted to talk," he said. "I was worried about you. That business with James, you got me scared. I never liked the guy, something wasn't right."

"I guess that makes you smarter than the rest of us," I said, and waited. One side of Stuart's collar was tucked into the neck of his sweater. I wanted to reach over and fix it.

Stuart leaned forward on the desk. "Also, congratulations. I helped Polly design the manager cards. You'll be great at this."

"We'll see what happens," I said. "I'm going to give myself some time to get things organized, then maybe later take a trip down to New York. I've never been there." Stuart wasn't going to talk about my performance at the Depot, and I was grateful for that.

"Really?" Stuart looked surprised. "You have to go to the Intrepid when you're there. You know, the sea, air, and space museum? You'd love it."

"Good idea," I said. I wondered how far this museum was from the garment district.

"Man, I wish I could go with you. Wonderful place," Stuart said, then caught himself and changed the subject. "What do you think you'll do here?" he asked, looking around at the debris of Rollie's tenure as manager. "Apart from the obvious housekeeping."

"I was thinking I should join the Chamber of Commerce," I said, surprising myself.

"Great idea, I'll sponsor you," Stuart said, the skin crinkling around his sailor's eyes. "Good time to sign up. Dinner meeting this month is ham and scalloped potatoes."

"As good as mine?" I asked, remembering a meal at my dining room table a few months, no, a lifetime ago. "Hold still," I said pulling the corner of the Oxford cloth collar free.

Stuart looked down at my hand under his chin and smiled again. "I doubt it, I'm pretty sure no one can match you."

The Agapi was crowded when I arrived for lunch. Darlene and Colleen were in the usual booth. When I walked in, it seemed to me for a minute the restaurant went quiet. Nick came up to me as soon as I sat down and very gently patted my shoulder. "What a terrible week. Lunch on the house."

I nodded my thanks. Colleen reached over and took my hands.

"Annette called us at Darlene's," she said. "In fact, I am pretty sure she called everyone. I know the whole story, but what I want to know is, how are you feeling?"

"At first, I was shaky," I said. "But now, I'm just mad. Who did James Martin think he was, coming here and doing this? Trying to pick up a part of our history and pretend it was his. It was all lies, to me, and to Rollie."

"I know, I know," Darlene said. "But it's over. You know, I'm proud of you. You never gave up, even though the Avon-from-antiquities necklace idea was a little out there. But you were trying to help us, to help Duck, I understand that. Plus," she looked at me in amazement, "you went out there

206

and confronted a killer. You're the only person I know who's ever done that."

"It's not something I'd recommend," I said, leaning back in the booth. Nick and Sophia both came and delivered our lunch. Judging by what was in front of us, they had decided to give us everything on the menu.

"What's this?" I asked, pointing to something unfamiliar on my plate.

"Ah, that? The new special." Nick rolled his eyes. "Kale spanakopita with vegan cheese. Very popular, for some crazy reason. George is going to put it on the food truck when he takes it down the beach."

"Very hungry, those surfers," said Sophia over her shoulder as she moved to the next table. "They'll eat anything."

When we were alone again, Darlene opened her purse. "Here, Mom," she said, fanning out brochures on the table between our plates. "These are for you. See how many interesting things you will be able to do once you move into town?"

Ignoring her, and the literature, Colleen picked up her coffee and began studying the picture of the Acropolis on the wall beside the table.

Darlene sighed. "Mom's in today to look at her new place," Darlene whispered to me. Colleen's eyes moved on to the Parthenon above the next booth. "It's just lovely, everything's going to fit. Smaller than the house, so Mom won't have so much work to do. I've been doing research for her on activities around here."

I picked up a brochure and started reading aloud. "Chair Yoga?" I looked at Colleen. "Computer skills for seniors?" "Bingo madness at the Legion?" "Eat right for one?"

"Thanks, Darlene," Colleen said, gathering up the pamphlets and jamming them forcibly back into Darlene's purse. "Great time passers I'm sure, if you have nothing better to do."

"Like what, Mom? At your age, it's important to stay engaged, all the studies say so. You're going to have time on your hands now."

I looked at across the table at Colleen and saw the woman who taught me how to sew and my mother's bridesmaid.

"She won't," I said, looking straight at Colleen. "I'm hiring her. As the new manager of Rankin's General, my first job is to get someone who knows what they're doing upstairs at the Co-op."

"That's right," Colleen said, sitting up straight in the booth, enjoying the look on her daughter's face. "Starting next week."

"Or sooner," I suggested, after a beat. "The inventory's piling up. How about the Thursday? Before the weekend rush?"

"I'll check my schedule. I'll see what I can do," Colleen said. "I want to get my nails done first."

Darlene opened her mouth, but no words came out.

"Deal," I said to Colleen, then, sensing that mother and daughter needed time to themselves to regroup, I stood up and walked over to the counter to thank our hosts for lunch. I settled in with the line of customers to wait my turn. Sophia was busy at the cash register, listening to a customer who, Nova Scotia–style, was describing her hysterectomy in great detail. George was near the window, serving charm and food to Kimberly, the thirsty jogger and tax collector, and Janice from Pittsburgh, aka Jennifer Fox.

I was beside the fish tank, a few feet from Sophia. The angelfish were drifting slowly around in the murky water, and the china castle was still slightly off-kilter. I thought I could see the dent in the colored gravel where the phone had landed not such a long time ago among the tinted rocks, pieces of glass, and polished gold beads.

I stopped breathing.

I looked over to the table at the window. George had his back to me, but I could tell from the rapt look on the faces of the two seated women that he was telling a story.

A very good story. An old story.

I absorbed the scene, then made a decision.

I leaned forward and rolled up my sleeve.

⌣ THE END ⌣

REFERENCES

Two books provided invaluable background for this story, and I highly recommend them both to any reader interested in either the true story of Operation Fish or the life of a real Nova Scotia rumrunner.

Draper, Alfred. *Operation Fish*. Don Mills: General Publishing Co. Ltd. Canada, 1979.

Miller, Don. *I Was a Rum Runner.* Yarmouth, N.S.: Lescarbot Publishing, 1979.

This classic is an excellent reference on the development of deception as a key element in the Allied war effort in WWII:

Cave Brown, Antony. *A Bodyguard of Lies*. New York: Harper Collins, 1975.

READER'S GUIDE

Crafting Deception
BY BARBARA EMODI

1. Events such as Operation Fish, the loss overboard of the *Fairyfox*, and Nova Scotia's rum-running history are woven into this story. Truth really can be stranger than fiction. What was your reaction to the fact that Churchill secretly sent the entire wealth of Great Britain across the Atlantic and that Roosevelt knew about it? Do you think a deception of this level could happen today?

2. The blue jays over Valerie's back door are a metaphor for some of what is happening in the story. Why does Val relate to them so strongly?

3. Valerie is struggling a bit to figure out the next stage of her life. If you were her best friend (in addition to Darlene) and could sit her down for a heart-to-heart, what would you say?

4. Sewing wedding dresses out of silk parachutes was common during WWII. Do you feel the women you know are still as resourceful?

5. Duck MacDonald is a simple man who is actually a complicated character. If you could write the next chapter of his life, what would happen? Could Duck ever become Stuart's rival for Valerie's affection?

6. The idea of Colleen's struggles to let go of her past and her possessions came to the author when she and her three sisters helped their mother move into assisted living. Have you ever had to help someone else move or declutter like this? What did that experience teach you, and how did it affect your own life?

7. The animals in the book—Toby the golden retriever, Shadow the cat, and even the mother blue jay and her nestlings—all have a message for the characters in this book. Can you think of what they are?

8. There are a number of objects from the past in this story that influence the lives of the present. In addition to the parachute, can you think of any others?

9. In their final confrontation, Val tells James, "You can't have anyone else's life; you only have the one that belongs to you. The only primary material is yourself." What do you think she means by that, and do you feel that it is an accurate statement?

10. How do you think the parachute really got into the basement, and what else is, or was, there? Where do you think it could be now?

11. Why do you think Valerie rolls up her sleeve at the end? What mischief is she going to get up to next?

ABOUT THE AUTHOR

Barbara Emodi lives and writes in Halifax, Nova Scotia, Canada, with her husband, a rescue dog, and a cat, who all appear in her writing in various disguises. She has grown children and grandchildren in various locations and, as a result, divides her time  between Halifax; Austin, Texas; and Berkeley, California, so no one misses her too much.

Barbara has published two sewing books—*SEW: The Garment-Making Book of Knowledge* and *Stress-Free Sewing Solutions*—and in another life has been a journalist, a professor, and a radio commentator.

Cozy up with more novels from best-selling authors...

FROM ANN HAZELWOOD

Wine Country Quilt Series

Door County Series

East Perry County Series

Colebridge Community Series

QUILTING COZIES BY CAROL JEAN JONES

Want more? Visit us online at ctpub.com